BARNABAS: RESTLESS FIGHTER

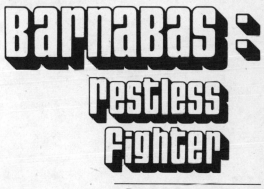

BARNABAS : restless fighter

John Warren Steen

BROADMAN PRESS
Nashville, Tennessee

ISBN: 0–8054–8702–6
4287–02

Library of Congress Catalog Card Number: 75–155683
Dewey Decimal Classification: F
Printed in the United States of America

To
my parents
Annabelle Henry Steen
and
John Warren Steen, Sr.

I.

Joseph kicked open the door and stepped into the smoky tavern. Discarding his sandals at the entrance, he shifted his bundle from his right arm to his left and hoped no one would ask questions about it.

Small pottery lamps, about the size of stepped-on pomegranates, glowed, turning the tables they were resting on into islands of light in a sea of darkness. The new arrival smelled burning oil, more pungent than the beverages. Joseph listened to the noisy groups gathered over the lamps but did not immediately recognize a familiar voice. He hoped he would not get into a fight on this last night before leaving Cyprus.

"Joseph, where have you been?" The words had been launched from a gambling table. As he walked toward the questioner, he saw a man without an ear.

"Looking for something." He felt an urge to tell the players about the smoldering unrest that made sleep difficult and the lust for travel that made settling down in one place impossible.

"Did you find it?" asked the one-eared gambler.

Joseph glanced at the stacks of bronze coins about the table and noticed that the smallest pile was in front of a man whose nose looked like an eagle's beak. "Yes, in a way. You might call me lucky." He decided not to tell them about his bundle's contents. "But I haven't found what I'm really searching for."

"You get some wrinkles in that smooth face of yours, and you'll find contentment in the process. You lose an ear, and I guarantee that you'll lose your restlessness. But wrinkles are easier and accomplish the same purpose. I recommend wrinkles."

Throwing his bundle over to a murky corner where someone had propped a Roman sword in a scabbard, Joseph ambled over to another table. He discovered some friends, whispering about rebellion against Rome, so intent on their conversation that they neg-

7

lected their drinks. The men, all in their early twenties, had once dressed regularly in their sabbath robes and gone to synagogue with Joseph, but now they wore old clothing, torn and frayed about the necks. He recalled his mother's question, "Why do you and your friends dress in that way? All of you can afford better garments. Is it because you want to flaunt our customs?" The words echoed in his mind as he listened to their complaints about Rome's laws, as well as God's laws. He heard one fellow bragging about the commandments he had broken and saw others leaning forward, ready to crow about their exploits. Then the youngest one saw him and shouted a welcome. Each one got up and grabbed him in a gesture of friendship.

"It's good to see you back."

"I'm not here for long. I sail from Cyprus tomorrow."

"Why don't you spend your life on this island? That's what we plan to do."

A companion named Eleazar, with his breath reeking, said, "If you refuse—you can leave if you want to—it seems that you don't trust our judgment—like you think you are better."

Before he could answer, the innkeeper stopped at the table long enough to wipe up some wine with his apron and added his advice, "Sailors tell me ours is the safest harbor in the empire. Stay here in Salamis."

"I know." Joseph quickly looked away toward the blackness of the wall and wished he could make them understand. "But I can't wait for something to come sailing here to me." He pulled up a chair and looked into the eyes of his acquaintances, which reflected the steady flame of the lamp in their stares. "I have to go out and prospect"—he didn't know whether they would understand his mining terminology—"you know, look for, search for—something."

The nose like a bird's beak pushed forward from the gambling table, and its owner said, "You should settle down here in Salamis. Be satisfied." It sounded like a threat.

Joseph asked for a drink. "What were you talking about when I came in?"

8

He listened as his cronies resumed their boasting. "Sure, I've eaten pork," said Eleazar, who had a remarkably red face.

"When?" demanded another.

"Some time back."

They argued that they had never seen him do it. The long-nosed man said, "I won't believe it until I see it. Eat some for us now."

Eleazar's face grew redder. "I'd rather . . . I don't care for the taste of it."

The outside door creaked open. As tavern customers glanced in that direction, their tongues stopped. Joseph was the last in the now-silent room to turn and notice a boy with a ragged tunic, too wide at the neck and exposing his left shoulder, standing there. Behind him loomed the enormous form of their rabbi, filling the doorway as if he were an angel of death. Joseph, knocking over his chair, stumbled to greet the visitor.

Fleshy jowls shook as the rabbi spoke, "Are you still going?"

"Yes, Rabbi."

"I will see you tomorrow at sunrise." The holy man, who had refrained from entering the place, stepped back, uncontaminated, and the boy slammed the door shut.

Everyone laughed. Joseph wondered how many men attended synagogue now. The red-faced man said, "Where are you going with that sack of grease?"

Joseph retreated from the doorway in the same way he had often approached the wrestling ring, deliberately but without haste. "Eleazar, don't poke fun at the rabbi or his religion."

"I'll tell you what I think of your rabbi. He looks so much like a pig, he must have had a sow for his mother."

Joseph slammed down his fist, sloshing wine onto the recently wiped table, and stood with his nose next to the nose of the braggart. Then he grabbed two fistfuls of Eleazar's robe, just below his chin, making it pull tight across his chest and back. "Do not say one word against that old man."

"I'll say what I please."

"Not as long as I am here to take up for him." Joseph twisted more tightly on the robe and let the constricting garment warn that

9

his wrestler's arms could squeeze out his opponent's breath in a few moments.

"Joseph," the red-faced man hissed between clinched teeth. When he received no answer but a tighter grip, he coughed and seemed hesitant. Someone from behind grabbed Joseph's shoulder. The former wrestler whirled around, still holding Eleazar with his left hand and sinking his right elbow into the assailant's stomach until he heard a groan. He saw that it was the bird-beaked man and expected further trouble from him. Still clinching Eleazar's robe with his left fist, Joseph used his powerful right arm to fling the moaning attacker across the room. He watched him reel and stumble, collapsing on the mysterious bundle of blankets and clothes in the shadowy corner. He felt a trembling beneath Eleazar's robe and sighed, reliving that moment of satisfaction he had always felt when a match was over and he could leave the ring, victorious and acclaimed.

The one-eared man who had left his table by the door, pushed his voice into the brief silence, "Joseph, you sound as if you were taking up for your own father."

"My father is dead." He started to say that the teacher meant nothing to him, but he simply added, "The rabbi and I are supposed to be leaving together on a trip."

"In that case," said the one-eared man, acting on an instinct of prevention that must have been bred from years of impulsive mistakes, "your friend here will say no more about your traveling companion. Is this not true, Eleazar?"

Joseph accepted the man's promise to say no more, and loosening his grip on the crumpled garment, watched him slink back to the corner near Joseph's valuable bundle. The long-nosed man whispered something. The two did not touch the roll of clothes and blankets. Joseph was ready; if they bent over to take the bundle, he would pounce on them and knock their heads together. He did not want to crack their skulls, but he planned to do so if it seemed necessary. However, they drifted toward the door. Eleazar paused long enough to call Joseph a gutter name and then left. Disregarding the insult, Joseph noticed the shadowy form of his pack but saw that the adjacent sword was missing.

An older man with a bald head said, "Have you turned to religion?"

The question was repulsive enough by itself, but the old fellow followed it with a high giggle, almost like a hen's cackle. Something boiled within Joseph, and he tasted an oath bubbling up in his throat, ready to be spat out at the jeering man. He doubled his fist. Nevertheless, a deep sadness seemed to paralyze his biceps. He did nothing, shaking his head in vigorous denial and pouring himself another drink. He had come to the tavern for many reasons, one of which was to find companionship in his loneliness. He had failed.

After Joseph had drained his cup, he spoke, "A religious man loses himself in his studies. I choose to lose myself in drinking. Pour me another."

Like returning waters of a high tide, activities swelled again—noisy gambling, whispered insurrection, and sloppy drinking. The reflections in Joseph's wine looked like a thousand campfires on a hill. He wanted to forget the fat rabbi. He wanted to forget even his trip at dawn.

There was a sudden increase of guffaws and shouts, and Joseph looked up to see two women carrying a pole to which was strapped a swaying sheepskin full of wine. The bleary-eyed man cheered as if they had been watching the final event of an Olympic game. He recognized the younger woman. She was a plump girl he had seen all his life, but he had never really noticed her. He could not have described what she was wearing, but he knew the garment did not come all the way up to her neck and was too tight around her chest.

After the women had deposited the skin, the plump one came toward Joseph's table. The woman smiled, and her bosom seemed to lift higher. He marveled that her dress could stand the stress. "You have the face of a boy," she whispered. As she said the words, she stepped backwards toward the night air of the courtyard. He could not keep from following her with his eyes. But the call of the wine was louder than the call of sensuality; so he lifted another cup of wine to his lips.

11

The room's heated odors stifled him; yet there was something safe about the place, like a mother's lap for a terrified child. No one mentioned the missing sword.

"There you are. I was looking for you." It was the innkeeper with the dirty apron. "This is your last chance to drink my wine for a long time, so I am giving you free drinks for the rest of the evening."

"What about us?" demanded a customer who was already drunk.

"When you prepare to leave Cyprus, I'll give you free drinking privileges, too—but not before. Besides, I want to leave a sweet taste in the mouth of this traveler. I think he'll return to us sooner than he expects."

Joseph, shaking his head, knew his desire to leave the island was like a thirst, and he ordered more drinks to assuage it. He wanted to discover what other people were like, what answers they had found. The racket of the room began to diminish to a hum, and his arm felt too heavy to move another cup to his lips. He could scarcely remember the rabbi or the wench or his trip. He passed into a stupor of smooth things, dreaming about rounded apples, sloping hills, and domed buildings. The night passed without his knowing that he was not in a bed.

A sharp feeling of discomfort awakened Joseph, but it took him a long time to get his thoughts cleared. He could not remember where he had gone to sleep, but he knew that his body felt tired all over. Then he concluded that his worst pain came from his head. There came a thumping in his back. He struggled to keep his eyes open and saw that a bare foot nudged him, not like a kick, but with a gentle insistence. "If you had been anyone else, I would have thrown you out." The owner, now dressed in a clean apron, seemed half amused.

Joseph sat up. He panicked about losing his bundle, until he found it where his head had rested. He longed to put his black curls back on the comfortable pack and sleep because tiredness saturated every muscle of his body.

"I'm grateful to you for letting me sleep here. If I ever have a floor of my own, you are welcomed to sleep on it."

The proprietor, tugging at Joseph's shoulders, trying to help him to his feet, said, "I hope that I will never have to spend a night away from my own bed and my own wife."

"I wonder," he sounded hoarse and stopped to clear his throat, "if I will live long enough to have a wife and home." Joseph could not have explained just what he meant by those words, and his voice rumbled as if it had tumbled down a distant mountainside. The tavern keeper was giving some sort of advice, as the young man, suddenly remembering the time for his proposed journey, lunged for the doorway, hooking his bundle with a sweep of his muscular right arm.

Joseph squinted his eyes as he stumbled out into the glare of a foggy morning. He saw two men resting beside the door. Half blinded and wondering if the ship had sailed without him, he walked more rapidly. The brilliant haze of fog was everywhere. A tree in a courtyard dripped moisture, and damp walls looked slimy. A dog trotted by, keeping his nose close to the street.

He glanced back and saw that the two figures reclining by the tavern entrance were now on their feet and moving in his direction. One was carrying a sword. Joseph wondered what odds a gambler would place on his life at that moment. He did not worry until he heard the shuffling of feet around the next corner. Could be a trap, he thought.

At the intersection leading to the dock, he met a group of individuals walking slowly, as if on their way to a funeral. The sun began crowding its way through the fog, and Joseph could see better the people and the street which ended at the warehouses beyond them. He recognized the peculiar limp and swing of the tailor's legs. Then he identified the olive oil dealer by his bald head. Next he recognized a stonemason. They were all members of the synagogue he had once attended. Separated from the group was a tanner, the same one who sometimes stood outside the synagogue window and longingly watched the services.

Running back and forth around the crowd, like an undecided puppy, was the boy who had walked with the rabbi to the tavern

13

and Joseph spoke a greeting of peace, *"Shalom,* Rufus." The child was wearing the same ill-fitting robe from the night before, with his shoulder still exposed.

"You picked a strange place to sleep." The boy in a tone lower than Joseph had expected from the vibrating chords in his young throat, said, "Take me with you. I want to see Jerusalem, too."

"I wish I could," said Joseph and gave him a hug. "Go back. The dock is no place for a child."

There was no response. Joseph sensed that the boy misunderstood him. He saw only the solemn gaze of wistful eyes. Their sadness matched the slowness of the cortege-like procession.

People moved ahead. The red-faced man with the sword followed the crowd; his companion was not visible. Then Joseph saw that the people were clustered around their aged teacher of the law, who was taking short, unsteady steps like a baby learning to toddle. My Rabbi, he thought.

The old man lumbered along, like a camel that makes a final trip, not carrying satins or spices like the others in a caravan, but without baggage heading for a place to die in some green oasis back home. Joseph shouted *Shalom* to the awkward man. "I hope we have not missed our ship."

The slow-moving individual said, "It was supposed to sail at daybreak, but I do not think the Lord will let it leave without me."

Joseph hoped the ancient one was right. Feeling the heat of the emerging sun on his tired shoulder muscles, he shifted his bundle. Over the heads of other people in the street and beyond the warehouse roofs, he could barely make out the masts of several ships, almost the same color as the lifting mist and perfectly still, without a bit of sway as far as he could tell.

As he hurried ahead of the group, the traveler heard one of the elders say to his rabbi, "Will you associate with that one?" He sensed that all the eyes in the group glared at the back of his head, as if he had been accused of some crime. He tried to appear unconcerned.

Joseph edged back to the critic. The man stepped aside to avoid being touched. Joseph whispered, "You should listen to the words

14

of that man because you are driving people away from the synagogue. I hope God strikes you dead." He called him the same name that red-faced Eleazar had called him the previous night.

"Rabbi, you can't get on the ship with that unclean man."

Their leader answered, loud enough for all to hear, "During the flood, the Almighty wanted animals of *every* kind in the ark."

Moving quickly toward the docks, he heard steps directly behind him and thought of the two disgruntled lawbreakers. When he glanced back, he saw that little Rufus was trotting to keep up with him.

As he started between two warehouse buildings, Joseph doubted whether they would be on time for the embarkation. Coming out on the wharf, which seemed unusually quiet, his heart began to pound as he saw a vessel out in the fog-shrouded harbor. "Where is that ship going?" he demanded of the nearest worker he saw on the dock.

"To Paphos, then to Rome."

He exhaled the worry that had built up within him and headed for a large ship that sat low in the water. It looked ready for sailing, perhaps in the other direction. The lines of its prow curved upward, and its bulwarks were touching the dock.

He looked across to see the captain of the vessel, inspecting the work of the deckhands. The man was dark and hardened, like a rock that had withstood many gales and rough seas, and the lines of his face recorded a history of many voyages. He looked as if he might have been descended from the ancient Phoenician seamen who had made the regular circuit from Byblos to Carthage to Tarshish. The commander of the vessel noticed Joseph's gaze and shouted at him, "Where have you been, you idiot?"

"I stayed up late getting some matters settled, and I must have overslept this morning. But it is rewarding to be welcomed aboard in such a cheerful way." He stepped on the sloping gangway, anxious for the voyage to begin.

The old teacher arrived at the gangplank, a few minutes later, puffing. Some of the younger men offered to carry him aboard, but he did not trust them.

15

Joseph, wanting to hurry the rabbi before the captain exploded, called out, "Come aboard," but hearing no grunt of response went back across the walkway and spoke louder. "It's time to leave for the promised land."

The old man spoke gruffly, "It will break my heart to leave." He turned his back to the ship, like a pouting child. Cruising gulls squawked overhead. No one spoke. Joseph paused for the accompanying elders to say something, and they waited for him. Someone needed to convince the balky man.

The hulking frame of the religious leader quivered with a sob, which brought an immediate response from the congregational leaders. One said, "You are our guide. We need you here."

"Yes," another added, "The only reason we allowed you to give up your work was for you to realize your dream of returning to Zion."

The captain's voice thundered, "All passengers, get aboard."

The old man dried off his cheeks, rotated his body toward the vessel, and without looking back, put his stronger leg on the short bridge that spanned the distance from land to vessel. He began his journey.

Joseph, turning to the elders, whispered, "He needed assurance that he was still wanted. That was the best thing you could have done for him."

Then Joseph heard the same one who had been critical, "Watch after him for us."

He answered, even though his head still felt pinched with pain, "I'll take care of him." Joseph, looking back one more time for some glimpse of Rufus, stepped on board the ship. He saw Eleazar and his crony with a beaklike nose slink away in disgust.

He watched the old man slowly trudge to the far side of the deck, away from the island and from the people on the quay. He saw him circle around like a dog making a nest in high grass and let himself collapse on the smooth boards of the deck. Joseph stood next to him to be his lookout. He told him the people on the dock were shouting their farewells and asking for his blessing. "They want you to wave to them."

16

"My work is over. They're no longer my flock."

"Rabbi! Just a moment ago, I watched you almost decide to stay here with them."

"It was a final temptation of Pharaoh before I started my exodus. Now I have crossed over."

Leaving the stubborn man, Joseph went to the rail and waved, hoping the people would interpret his farewell as the good wishes of their spiritual guide. Then he turned to a sailor, "How soon will we leave?"

"Only the Fates know. We can't leave until papers are signed for our return cargo." Joseph laughed when he thought of the captain's blaming them for the delay.

The vessel seemed ready for her cruise. The anchors were up, and the hatches were on. Two sailors waited high up the mast on the yardarm, checking the rigging, ready at any moment to do their part to release the great square sail that would billow down to the boom and capture the windpower that the Fates or heaven or God had sent for them to use in propelling the craft to its destination.

During the day, Joseph watched the loading of a lead-sheathed ship, which he guessed was heading for Rome. Stevedores lugged sacks of wheat on board from the warehouses. Once during the delay, Joseph spied his little friend wandering back up the road toward a fishing community. Others of the congregation on the dock drifted away to their affairs. Ones who remained sat on wooden boxes or pieces of broken masts in the twilight, prepared to wait out the delayed embarkation.

At sunset small boats began to return to harbor. He saw a swift moving lateen, with its slanting mast and triangular sail, glide right up between their vessel and the lead-sheathed grain ship. Other little fishing craft tied up together out near the end of the jetty. It seemed to be a time for coming in, not for leaving.

A messenger came aboard and left. Then, with a single order bellowed from the captain, the ship pulled away. Suddenly, there was a golden stretch of water between the boat and the wharf. After the long, tedious wait, the actual embarkation had come abruptly.

Joseph heard the shrill call of a child, "Come back." He waved,

17

but the cry grew more desperate. He longed to go to Rufus and hold him, explaining why he had to leave Cyprus and why he must explore Judea. He wanted to stand by the little orphan. The siren cries continued. Joseph now comprehended stories he had heard of an enticed captain ordering his men to lash himself to the mast to keep from jumping overboard. Regrets began to squeeze his throat until he felt he was choking. He wished that he could break down and sob like the old rabbi had done at the gangplank, and maybe then he, too, would be cleansed of his grief.

He looked back toward Cyprus and saw it dwarfed by mountainous clouds of slate gray with seared edges. As the coastline of the lovely island turned into a hazy dream and the craft began to dive into the dark swells of the sea, the two travelers reached out for each other with words. It had been months since Joseph had conversed with a religious person, and he said uneasily, "The night looks blessed for travel."

The other one agreed and began to tell about the fine weather in the holy land. Speaking slowly and with great authority, he expounded certain Scriptures that mentioned weather. As the vessel rose and dipped, with its timbers creaking, he brought his exegesis to a close with a comparison of the providential weather to that of Cyprus. "It is not like an island in the sea, which is subject to a storm from any direction. The weather there is as dependable as her Lord, even though he might afflict his people with an earthquake or a drought once or twice in a generation." The listener yawned.

Afraid that the old man might launch into a new lecture on the judgments of God, Joseph got up to walk about the deck. It was not large, yet ample; it looked clean enough to lie on in his best sabbath robe. The captain stopped him. "This is not a pleasure ship. We cannot be inconvenienced by the whims of the passengers."

Joseph wondered whether the rude man with the lined face was objecting to his stroll over the deck but decided he was concerned over other matters. "We were on board ship long before you weighed anchor. Don't blame us for the delay."

18

"I am not speaking of that. I simply don't want any trouble from the old man. He looks too feeble to attempt such a trip."

"He's stronger than he looks."

"Why did he change his mind back there?"

"Did you never change yours at the last minute, when you felt it was your last chance to turn back from something terrifying, such as entering a harbor in a storm or taking a wife?"

Grim lines in the face of the seafaring man cracked into amused wrinkles, even visible in the starlight. "They're alike, I admit." Then the deep lines returned in all their rigidity. "But I have always known what I wanted and never wavered."

Joseph thought, I will be determined like that if ever I can decide what I want.

The captain said, "We don't provide meals for passengers."

"We brought our own."

"If anything happens to that old man, I will not turn back. I cannot stop this ship. We are late. I will not even stop for a burial at sea."

"You will not have to. I will take care of his meals." Joseph threw back his shoulders and boasted, "The God he believes in will watch out for his health."

"It sounds like you, too, believe he will protect the old fellow," the captain grumbled, as he returned to his command post. Joseph let the words flow over him unnoticed, like spray from the prow, as he returned to his fellow traveler.

He helped the feeble man to the hatchway and preceded him down the ladder, helping to pull him through the small opening, patiently enduring the time it took. The old man grumbled that his bunk was too narrow, and Joseph was disappointed that his own was too short to stretch out in. The grumbling stopped, and the great man began a night of wheezes and snores.

Next morning they struggled back up to the fresh air and ample space of the deck. The rabbi said that he was too sore from the previous day's walk to the boat to want any further exercise. Joseph moved about the ship. Near the stern, he talked with one of the helmsmen who was steering by the rudder. He learned little from

19

the ignorant man, but he was thankful the clod knew enough to direct the craft in a southeasterly direction.

Returning to his companion, he began to feel again the need to talk. "Do you think a man can lengthen his days?"

"Yes, the commandment promises it to the nation that honors its parents."

"I have no father, but I have tried to honor my mother."

"By leaving her alone?" he asked, making Joseph sorry that he had asked. Then the rabbi probed, "Are you running away from her?"

Joseph looked back toward the bubbly wake of the ship. "She knows that I am leaving." The conversation had made him concerned about the brevity of life, but he did not care to mention the fact to the teacher again. He didn't want to confess. He didn't want further advice.

"Was it hard for you to leave your mother?"

"No, I left her two years ago." He stared at the horizon and recalled the shrinking outlines on the dock. He hesitated for a moment and then said, "I hated to leave Rufus."

"Why did you torture yourself into making this trip?"

"I had to come." Salty spray hit his forehead, and he wiped it off with his hand. "I cannot explain it."

The old man appeared to be waking up from a deep sleep, looking and sounding rested. "God gives people hunger to know they need food. He gives them thirst to know they need wine, a small amount, you understand. He has given you a longing to find yourself and your destiny." He paused and added, "Your mission, your goal. You must endure this hunger until you discover something satisfying."

Joseph doubted it but did not say so. Yet he could not get the thought out of his mind. As he watched the sailors, he tried not to ponder his purpose in life. He listened to the chief mate, swearing and commanding the ship's company to bestir themselves. Some were splicing rope. Others were scrubbing decks. A few were making minor adjustments to the sails or rigging. Still the dreaded thought lingered, and he returned to the religious teacher.

20

His place on the deck was empty, although the unguarded bundle was there. He wondered if the dotterer could have stumbled overboard. He raced below decks and found him in the cramped sleeping quarters.

Joseph was not ready to sleep. Back on deck he looked out at the silvery trail ahead. The ship was a great, rocking cradle, but he could not sleep. He watched the horizon for some answer to his yearning heart—not just for a glimpse of land, but for some reward, some prize, some answer, some miracle.

While sailors below were swilling their morning victuals, the two Cypriots climbed the ladder-like steps to the deck. The younger one went first, reaching back to help the rabbi, who never stopped talking, but between words gulped air like a caught fish. "This," he panted, "is a strange trip."

"Yes, it is strange," said Joseph, who offered a supporting arm. He did not care to stay on the subject. "We should land within a couple of hours." He helped the old man trudge over the swaying deck and sit on a coil of rope. He threw down his own blanket-wrapped bundle, which he purposely had not opened during the trip, not even during the two chilly nights.

Then, satisfied with their isolation, Joseph unwrapped the meal of properly prepared salt fish. "What would you like to eat?" he asked, as if he possessed the menu of a Roman banquet inside his folded cloth. The captain glared at them.

"Nothing," the old man mumbled.

"You will eat when we get there. I know you will."

There was only a muttered answer like humming and then an unaccustomed quiet. He offered the old man some diluted wine from his traveler's flask, but the offer was rejected. "Afraid of sea sickness?"

"No," he smiled. "I have no need for food."

Joseph squinted his eyes for a better look at the rabbi and wondered if he had refused because of a religious fast or simple stubbornness. The man had been a riddle to him, but he asked no embarrassing questions because the voyage was almost over.

Something about the patriarch reminded him of a pig, although

21

the idea earlier had made him angry enough to fight. The lawabider had never tasted pork and had probably never been near a hog. It was not so much his actions, although he snorted a little, at times, and rolled his eyes about in their sockets of flesh. It was the fat—the abundance of fat—that reminded Joseph of a pig. Billows of fat rolled over his cheeks and down his neck below his robe. He looked like a pregnant sow, sluggish and bloated.

"I never thought we would celebrate this day on board ship," Joseph said briskly. It was the first day in the month of Tishri, when Jews mark the beginning of the new year, a time for celebrating the creation of the world. He was as fretful as a hungry child and began to pace back and forth. Joseph paused to look for land to appear on the horizon. While he stood at the ship's wooden railing, he plowed his thumbnail into the piece of polished wood, carving a furrow that matched the one going across his brow. The trip was not something he wanted, like a man wants a woman, but was something he felt driven to do, more like a boy fights to protect his mother's name.

"This is a strange trip for both of us," the seer repeated. Joseph agreed. It was odd to be traveling with a man he had hardly glimpsed for the past two years, a man so dissimilar in age and outlook. "I can leave Cyprus. It is not my home, but it is yours."

"Do Jews ever have a home anywhere?" asked Joseph cynically.

"Jews!" The venerable teacher sighed, "I wish we were landing in Joppa, where there are more of God's people."

Joseph did not argue. "I know that you don't like Caesarea, but seamen say the port facilities there are better."

Joseph, himself, was disappointed, but not for the same reason. He had never before been to Jerusalem, even though both his parents had come from the place, and he had heard enough about it to draw a map of the Holy City before he was twelve. He had planned to be there for the High Holy Days, which were already beginning. He could not explain his plans; he had never observed the law strictly, even though his widowed mother and the rabbi had been insistent. He had planned to be in the Temple on this day, to hear the ram's horn proclaiming the new year and to listen to the antiphonal choirs of Levites. He wanted to mingle with excited fanatics and frenzied celebrants in the Holy City, hoping that their enthusiasm might become contagious.

A sailor sighted land and another took soundings. "Twenty fathoms," he chanted, sounding much like the cantor who used to thrill their synagogue with his singing talents.

"Get off the lines," a seaman commanded, and Joseph lifted the rabbi over to a clear space on the deck.

"I feel like Moses, looking over into the promised land and seeing it occupied by uncircumsized heathen," said the rabbi, and Joseph respected his strictness.

As the harbor towers of Caesarea became visible, sculptured and symetrical in the cloud-crowded dawn, Joseph tried to identify the sites the old teacher pointed out. To the north of the harbor, he spotted the aquaduct with its repeated arches, like continuing waves on the ocean yet bringing sweet water from the distant Carmel range. Then to the south he saw the theatre. "Not quite as large as ours in Salamis, but in a more beautiful setting, with the Mediterranean as a natural backdrop," said the young man. Satisfied that they were not talking about his personal life, he tried to get his hands to relax as he listened.

The rabbi said, "Herod the Great built almost everything you see. He discovered that the people of Jerusalem would never share his love for coarse drama and gladitorial games; so he established his residence here. He tried to build a little Rome; you can see how well he succeeded." They sailed nearer the breakwater, where waves that had started rolling near Spain crashed against the jetty with volcanic-like explosions.

Like a bird that follows some inward direction to migrate, Joseph felt pulled toward his destination. Some instinct, some shadow of an idea, some echo of a thought compelled him to visit the promised land. He believed that it held for him some promise.

"My son, hold your hands still." The rabbi spoke as if he were

23

scolding a schoolboy, but, obediently, Joseph folded his hands behind him and tried to keep from squeezing first one and then the other. "You know, Joseph, you talk like your hands move, fast and agitated. Try to slow down."

The captain cursed and said he wanted them out of the way. Joseph made a curt reply and turned to his companion. "I want us to start moving as soon as we dock. Maybe we can find an ass for you to ride, but I expect to carry my bundle a long distance today."

"What do you have in the bundle?"

Joseph unclasped his nervous hands and threw them up, fingers stretched wide apart, to quieten the questioner before he alerted the whole greedy crew. "My life, really."

The old man nodded, as if he comprehended, and a large flock of gulls coasted overhead. Presently, below deck, someone threw out a pail of slop, and the birds, shrieking and chirping, swooped down to pick up a free meal from the frothy wake. The lecturer continued to describe the promised land.

"Old Herod wanted a great port; so he selected this unlikely beach. He ordered vast stones more than fifty feet in length, and not less than eighteen in width, to be let down into the water. These formed a great seawall in the shape of a semicircle. Do you realize that this harbor is larger than Athens' port of Piraeus?" The talkative teacher began to slow down, but he did not pause for an answer. "One of the mysterious sites of Caesarea is the villa of Pontius Pilate, but you will never get to see it. That moody despot has it surrounded with double security, as if he were under siege."

"You know a lot about this place you dislike."

The aged man sighed, "Cornelia has told me about it." He explained nothing more to curious Joseph about the place or the informer but sat there silently, while noisy seagulls circled overhead.

"We will not pause there long, and then we . . ."

"Do not expect me to go on to Jerusalem with you." The words sounded alien in the rabbi's throat, as if spoken by a *goy*, a Gentile. It would not have seemed surprising to Joseph to hear the words

24

coming from his own lips, which were frequently bitter, sometimes profane. Even at that moment he wondered why he was heading for a holy place. The elder continued, "I knew I had to tell you, but I thought I could wait. I will give you my reason after we disembark."

During the long wait outside the harbor, Joseph, stunned, leaned against the rail. He could look down into the transparent green water. He could see sand on the ocean floor but no marine life. He did not see what he looked for, and he wondered if he also might find nothing on the lonely trip to Zion. The thrill he had experienced earlier changed. His excitement at sighting the land of Israel turned into a terror of the unknown that caused him to curse, "Great God!" The teacher hearing it, shook his jowls in agreement, as if it had been a prayer.

At the last possible moment, the crew struck sail, and Joseph watched as oars from portholes below deck hit the polished surface with frothy splashes. The vessel moved slowly toward the narrow entranceway to the dock, and on each side of the opening he saw a colossal statue mounted on a barnacle-encrusted pillar. He wondered how long it would take him to discover the identity of Cornelia.

II.

The quay was swarming with workers stripped to the waist. Some of these dock workers waited to catch ropes hurled to them from the ship and to secure the lines. One of them yelled a question about the cargo to anyone aboard who would answer.

"Marble columns from Italy," came the reply. The answer produced several sneers and grunts of disapproval on the wharf.

After the captain stepped ashore with his wharfage fee in hand, the exhausted ship vomited out its passengers and most of its crew on to the busy dock. Joseph threw his baggage to his right shoulder and hoped people would think it was simply his bedroll. He offered his left arm for his feeble comrade to lean on. They were the last ones to leave the ship. It inconvenienced no one when the rabbi paused on the gangway to shake from his sandals the dust from a heathen island and a Gentile vessel. He wished not to pollute the sacred soil.

They found the area in front of the multiple-arched warehouses an anthill of activity. Heathen Caesarea was taking off no time to celebrate the Jewish New Year. There was no elation and no penitence. Growling stevedores continued loading some vessels and unloading others.

The heavy man headed for an eddy in the flowing stream of workers. He pushed toward a litter made of polished wood, resembling a bed with posts at each corner and a covered frame overhead. Oddly, the rabbi headed straight for that symbol of idle luxury deposited in the work area of muscle-strained workers. It rested on the paved quay, guarded by four slaves in fresh tunics. As the slow traveling companions reached that spot, a woman stepped from the resting litter and said, "I will take my father." Jewels clung to her neck and hung from her ears. Around her eyes were lines of soot black in the ridiculous custom of Egyptian women.

Joseph shook his head. He looked to his aging friend for some

26

denial of this unbelievable revelation. He remembered how the rabbi had told him about the architecture of Caesarea but had omitted any reference to the identity of his source. Now he heard the old man verify the painful fact, "This is my daughter, Cornelia. She lives here."

She stared at Joseph but said nothing to him. Instead, to her father she spoke, "We brought three donkeys, one for you to ride on and two others to carry your baggage. We can send back for anything else later."

The rabbi held up his palms, "I gave everything away. My needs are simple."

"How childish."

Joseph hugged the old man. At that moment, he forgot differences of age and temperament; he would have made any sacrifice to save his friend from suffocating in an atmosphere of misunderstanding and irreverence. He said, "Come with me to Jerusalem."

"No, my young friend, I am too weak."

Joseph wished that the older man had prepared him for this lightening-bolt development. He had heard him talk so much and say so little that he had been forced to fill in the gaps with his own guesses. He had presumed that the rabbi's daughter lived in Jerusalem and that they would travel on to the Holy City together. As slaves helped the old man to the back of a donkey, Joseph stepped nearer the woman and asked for information he had to know, "Are you married to a Roman?" He knew that a scrupulous observance of the law would no longer be possible for a Jewish rabbi living under the same roof with a *goy* and eating from the same dishes.

"That is none of your business." Her few remarks to him had been haughty and defensive. Abruptly, an overtone of kindness vibrated in her voice. "Here are two donkeys. They are yours in payment for the help you have given my father."

The ancient one on the other donkey said, "Yes, Joseph has been patient with me. He has been like a son."

Joseph, becoming embarrassed at her unexpected kindness, offered to accept one of the animals if she would let him buy it. He would not receive it as payment for doing what he knew was his

27

duty.

She refused payment and said, "Very well, take this strong one, Olivia. I will lend her to you."

Joseph, glad to have an excuse to return to Caesarea to visit his old friend, accepted the loan. "How can I find you to return Olivia?"

"Everyone in Caesarea knows my place as the House of the Laughing Satyr. It is next to the temple of Artemis."

References to paganism, bubbling casually from her lips, again provoked grave doubts in his mind. Blaming himself, he felt like a judge who had just condemned an old man to death. He wondered if he would ever again see his teacher alive.

He took the rabbi's hand and kissed it. His voice was too full to talk. Joseph picked up his bundle of clothing, threw it over the donkey's back, and led her up from the dock toward the east. Without wasting time to ask questions about the road to Jerusalem, he instinctively took the main street that bordered the forum and then headed east past the hippodrome. There was something hopeless about the situation—a cutting of roots and a dislodging of life. Thus, torn out of familiar relationships and unattached, Joseph needed a home, and his heart cried out for the courts of the living God. Perhaps, he fervently hoped, he could find some meaning to life in Jerusalem.

The old fellow had been a constant concern during the entire trip, and now Joseph's thoughts, by habit, remained on him. He had nursed the rabbi on board ship, and now he could do nothing for him but grieve. Years ago, despite the evident barriers, the older man had seemed approachable to adolescent Joseph. He had developed a loving respect for the rabbi, even though at the synagogue he had never been able to keep his mind on the scholar's lengthy interpretations of the law. He had gladly run errands, fetched fuel, and occasionally helped in the synagogue services.

The horny hoofs of the ass struck the paving stones in loud claps. Otherwise, there was silence. "The days of our past are dead," said Joseph, half aloud. He considered turning back to rescue the rabbi from his spiritual prison, but he knew such action was foolish. Like

28

the Babylonian captives, the rabbi had resigned himself to reality.

Joseph missed his friend and planned to return soon, perhaps after ten days, following the Day of Atonement, to check on his welfare.

During the afternoon, Joseph became so desperate for conversation that he began talking to Olivia. He had not spoken with anyone since he had left the wharf. If he could find no one else, he would still speak to the ass—unworried about her telling anyone.

"On this special day, when the hours of the night and day are exactly equal, I had wanted to be in the Temple court. I had planned to see the opening of the east gate, when the first rays of the sun, rising over the Mount of Olives, shone across the court, over the great altar, and between the two glistening pillars into the holy place of the Temple." Joseph mused over the many stories he had heard about the New Year from his mother. Then, realizing that he had slowed down to a funeral pace, he walked faster. "But my main hope now is to get there safely, even if I am late, and to keep my treasure out of the hands of robbers."

Joseph found talking with the donkey unsatisfying. He longed to hear a response to his hopes or to find some reassurance when he mentioned his fear. He ceased talking and tried to get his mind off the danger.

On this important road linking Syria and Egypt, he had expected to see more traffic. No one was heading in his direction. He guessed that all the pilgrims had gone on to Jerusalem previously to find lodging and to prepare for the holy days. Only a herdsman with his stinking goats passed in the other direction going toward Caesarea.

He counted several milestones before the paving stopped. Joseph did not fret. If he had been driving a chariot or a wagon, he would have missed the paving stones. The road at this point was still under construction, with only a hard surface foundation. Walking beside his donkey, he had concerns other than the highway's condition. Joseph hoped that this thoroughfare was not infested with robbers.

Along the parched road that had felt no caress of rain for six months, Joseph noticed a dust cloud formed by two distant figures running. He trembled. Fear was an unusual emotion for Joseph. He was a strong man, taller than the average Jew. He was energetic. He knew how to protect himself if he needed to, for he had learned wrestling in the gymnasium at Salamis. Suddenly, the two distant figures disappeared.

During the afternoon, Joseph came to a flimsy wooden bridge over a small stream. He could tell from the steep banks that in the rainy season this trickle of water became a destructive flood. Nearby he saw a collection of stones, fresh-quarried, ready to be engineered into an enduring bridge. He threw himself down on the hard, sandy soil that was the color of a rusty nail. He allowed Olivia to drink and rest. He knew that she could relax better with her burden removed, so he rose and untied it from her back. Joseph looked at the conglomeration of blankets, robes, and rugs and wondered if anyone could guess what was sewed inside. He had never before possessed as much. He felt insecure. What had taken so long to accumulate could be lost instantly!

Then, like some dreaded prophecy coming to pass, he felt his arms seized from behind and held by long bony fingers. A piercing chuckle was echoed by Olivia's nervous braying. The arms holding his were small, like a girl's, and he knew he would have no trouble breaking loose. However, he felt the prick of a dagger blade against his throat and saw that it was held by a second ruffian, a man with deep holes gouged into his complexion by some childhood disease.

"When you pass through Samaria, expect to meet Samaritans," the rough-faced man snickered.

"When you meet a Jew from Cyprus, expect a fight," Joseph warned.

"If you fight with us, you will get yourself killed."

"I have nothing to lose; my life is worth nothing." He snapped his knee upward and kicked the robber all the way over to Olivia, who in turn did her part, adding her kick to Joseph's. The dagger had fallen into her excrement, and the robber swore as he soiled his hands to retrieve it. Joseph whirled around and grabbed the

30

other man from behind. He looked undernourished and wore a scraggly blond beard which partially covered his sunken cheeks. The Cypriot felt that he could break the man's arm or even his neck without exerting all his energy, but just at that moment, the bearded one slipped from his hold and drew a dagger even longer than his companion's blade that had so recently been at his throat. The two thieves, holding their weapons like swords, went to the bundle and began rummaging through the cloaks and rugs, seeing what would fit their needs. At a safe distance, Joseph watched as they came to the cloak that was sewn together and saw them rip it open and put their dirty hands on his golden coins.

"We are rich." He knew there were one hundred and twenty coins, although they did not stop to count the hoard. "What are you doing with them? Where did you steal them? Is anyone following you?"

Joseph spat on the ground at the idea. "I would go hungry before I would steal." He was not afraid, not nearly as worried as he had been on the lonely road not knowing what to expect.

"How then did you get so much gold?" asked the emaciated one.

He decided to recall for them the chain of circumstances that had produced the money. His father had left him a small pasture land. He had worked for two years to pay for an adjoining pasture where sheep could be grazed. He wanted more land. Then he had been able to accumulate another parcel in exchange, when he swapped his best horses to a man who was moving to another part of the island. He had wanted to be a part of the island, and he thought that owning land would give him a feeling of participation. He did find a measure of security, but not the feeling of belonging he desired. He was a Jew living on a Greek-colonized island ruled by the empire of Rome. He did not actually belong to the island, and he felt like an eagle that had paused only for a rest in a treetop far from home.

The pair listened carefully, and he inched closer to them, confident that he would be able to overpower the two before they could use their lethal blades to slit his throat or chop into his chest. The recounting, like a charm, was casting a spell of unwary disregard over the robbers. At the same time, Joseph realized it was giving him a kind of pleasure, a type that he had long denied himself—a satisfaction of recall, a reliving of happy times, a felicitous sharing even with two emaciated Samaritans.

Joseph recalled that he had entered marriage with more security than he had ever felt before. During the distrubing years between his *bar mitzvah* and his engagement, he yearned for the contentment of finding a responsive Jewish mate and rearing a large household of Jewish children. He longed for the experience of fatherhood, when he could say that with God's help he had produced a man-child. He wanted to pass along his family name. He wanted to give his children a love for God, and he wanted to teach them to take care of the land which the Creator had given them. There was something ludicrous about the tale-telling, with grown men listening to the kind of love story that women whisper about when they go to the well. Also, it seemed to Joseph, it was pitiable—their longing to hear about the life of a man whose race despised them. It seemed ironic to listen pleasantly to one from whom they were about to seize his dearest possessions. And it was sad, almost tragic, for him to be squandering the loveliest memories of his life on wicked half-breeds. Despite the tragic and ridiculous aspects of the encounter, he continued, neglecting to creep any closer for the moment.

"Those months of married life—ten of them, only ten months— they were the happiest of all my years. I no longer felt a restlessness. Things seemed settled. I had accomplished something, but God took it all away." His eyes rekindled the glow of contempt that had been focused on the highwaymen. "The Almighty took my wife in childbirth." He refused to pause over the calamity. "Afterwards, I had no interest in land. What happened to it was no concern of mine. I wanted to leave it."

The bitterness of the memories aroused the storyteller to his present danger, and he began to move closer to his listening foes. He recalled for them the memory that came to his grief-pounded mind. Hoping to get over his sorrow, he had swapped the land with its stabbing memories for a plot in the mountainous regions near the north-central portion of the island. On his first visit to his new property, like some ancestor from chalcolithic times, he had stooped down to pick up a lump of reddish dirt. He had found it strangely heavy. He, like his ancient predecessor, had pounded it and found that instead of splitting it spread out. The ancestor had discovered this pounding to be an easier method for making knives, weapons, and scythes than chipping them from flint. Joseph easily identified the metal as copper, because Cyprus had many such mines. Indeed, the island's very name had come from copper. Then Joseph discovered another piece covered with a delicate green patina. He knew more about the metal than his predecessors, who had lived in caves. He knew that the ore could be melted and the soft metal shaped into utensils. Also, he knew of the ancient discovery of adding one part of tin to nine parts of copper. The mixture would become bronze. Since Rome was requiring more and more bronze for armor, swords, axes, and sculpture, he could sell it for a handsome amount.

Regardless of the profit, he had not wanted to part with the land. It made him feel a part of Cyprus. Yet, he found an insistent buyer, a wealthy owner of another mine, who wanted to expand his holdings. Without magic, Joseph had been able to turn one metal into another. Copper produced his gold. He was given one hundred and twenty pieces of gold as an initial payment, with the promise of more as the mine produced.

Once he had the money, he felt that he must use it in the homeland of the Hebrews. Somehow the investment could prepare a place for him in God's special land, where he could send down roots. He desired to belong, as much as the smallest lamb of the biggest flock wants to be a part of the herd. Now Joseph was heading for Jerusalem to discover how he could become a part of God's chosen people who were living in the Promised Land.

The thin robber with the beard chanced to glance down the road and hissed, "Do you know this soldier coming?" All three men saw an erect figure, mounted and stirring up little puffs of dust, coming on the road from Caesarea.

"No," the Cypriot answered.

"You lie. He will see us crucified if he . . ." They dropped the gold, the bundle, and ran along the wadi bank to safety in the hills.

The value of the copper, which God had taken years to bring to maturity, almost had been lost in a moment to God's purposes. Joseph began to straighten the pack, to make it look as inconspicuous as possible. He recognized that the traveler was a Roman soldier on an Arabian stallion. He watched him dismount and walk toward the stream. "Where are you heading?" the stranger demanded, oblivious of the escaping robbers, whom Joseph was satisfied to forget.

"Jerusalem, and you?"

"Same destination. Here, go with me."

Joseph knew the law. He could be compelled to go a mile with the soldier. Whatever baggage impeded the soldier, he could be made to carry. Joseph resented the military order, but he was so relieved the stranger was not another robber that he showed no grudge.

They returned to the road. "Why do you not ride on the donkey?" the Roman asked.

"I prefer to walk and let her carry the load."

In a voice accustomed to giving commands, he said, "Let her carry both you and the load."

"I want to be fair," Joseph said firmly. He saw the soldier's disapproval folded in lines on his brow, but he watched the wrinkles relax as the man dismounted also. Joseph guessed that the Roman soldier was about his own age. He wondered why the stranger was trying to sound important.

Leading the horse by its bridle, he walked alongside Joseph. "Do you live around here?" he asked.

"No, I come from Cyprus."

"What news do you hear from Rome?"

Joseph expected this common question. Every soldier wanted to know what headquarters was doing. Here in this distant province, news was slow in arriving and eagerly received.

"The ship on which I took passage came from Rome. The captain said that Emperor Tiberius still isolates himself on the Isle of

34

Capri. He decides many military and political matters on the basis of astrology. If the stars are not in a satisfactory positon, he will not make strategic moves, regardless of how much assurance there is for victory."

"Perhaps he sets an example for the rest of us. We have tried every other belief, and they are all equally disappointing."

"Indeed, all is disappointing except worshiping the one true God and living by his law." He surprised himself with the pious answer.

"You sound like the Jews that I met in Alexandria."

Joseph deflected the point of the conversation. "Yes, there are many Jews there."

"True, there are many, and they have given up any silly insistence on the Hebrew language. They even use a Greek translation of their law and Scriptures." Joseph was familiar with such attitudes from his associates in Cyprus. When he said nothing, the soldier started over. "I am Julius of the Augustan Cohort. I have just come form Egypt on a grain ship. I landed at Caesarea with orders for Herod's garrison, and then I go on to Syria. You see, I am an imperial courier."

"I am Joseph of Salamis. I had hoped to be in Jerusalem for today, but at least I can be there for 'the day.' "

He asked, "What day?" Any Jew would have known the answer.

"The Day of Atonement, our only holy day of fasting." Joseph had admitted the obvious fact of his race.

Each man stared at the other, curious. Joseph smiled and admitted his question. "How do you happen to be alone on this road?"

"I usually never travel alone. But my companion got sick on board ship, and I left him with the military police at the harbor."

The two travelers continued to talk for the remainder of the afternoon. On a lonely trip with a stranger he would never see again, Joseph spoke freely. He told him how it felt to be a Jew living on an island of paganism. When he finally stopped talking, he felt exhausted, but as cleansed as if he had come from the baths.

35

In the last afterglow of day, when the sun had already disappeared, they noticed a building, larger than an ordinary dwelling, located just off the road. They found that it was a caravanserai, where they could stay overnight. In the common room, they ate a meal of lentils, cucumbers, and chick-peas and then retired for the evening. They placed their animals in the inner courtyard and slept in stalls beside them. The only óther guest was a camel driver who snored. His four camels and their own animals were quiet during the night, but Joseph woke up several times with the feeling that vermin were crawling over him. With the first cock crow before sunrise, he was ready to continue the journey and awakened Julius.

During the morning they passed fields of scorched grasses and weeds. Everything was a faded yellow, except the enduring blue of the star thistle, whose blossoms were dried and dead, but still a brighter hue than the sky. When they came to the town of Antipatris, they stopped for some fig cakes and light wine. They left the town with dogs barking after them and soon were a distance from the Sharon Plain. The road led gradually upward through an ascending valley.

The Roman cleared his throat, and Joseph expected a question about the contents of his baggage. The soldier said, "You can tell this road has been planned by the Romans. Notice how the elevation increases gradually. There is only a slight variation up or down and only the most necessary deviation from side to side as the terrain dictates." He sounded like a long-winded senator.

Joseph could not keep from smiling. He knew the Romans had surfaced the road and set up frequent milestones, but he guessed that this had been a footpath centuries before when Abraham brought his family and flocks into the land. He presumed that it had been widened during the time of King Solomon, so that royal chariots could easily travel it. Yes, he thought, the Romans might have straightened out a few curves, but the highway had Jewish foundations.

While he was thinking about the people who had traveled this road, Julius' conversation, like a fox chasing a rabbit, went in another direction. He suddenly asked, "What is the purpose of marriage?" Without waiting for a reply, he continued, "Please do not say for the purpose of having children. Reproduction does not depend on matrimony. Why marry?"

Joseph answered, "After God created the world, he called good everything he created except a bachelor. He said, 'It is not good that man should be alone.' He made a companion for him."

"That story is about as fanciful as the legend of Romulus and Remus being suckled by a she-wolf."

"No," said the Jew, "the main point in the creation story is just as true of marriage in this era. Marriage should be an enduring companionship. This is what brings satisfaction, not physical desire which is just . . ."

"Then tell me what went wrong with mine. I married a patrician girl of eighteen, and she expected me to continue to spoil her with gifts as her foolish father had. She lived for entertainment. By Jupiter, I have never seen a person search so hard for pleasure. Whenever I left Rome on a business venture, she looked for entertainment in places where it was easy to find. Finally, I sent her back to her silly father and left for the foreign service. I doubt that I can trust any woman now."

"I cannot speak for other marriages, but I know that my own was a happy one. The most glorious ten months of my life were spent while I had a wife."

"Where is she now?" the Roman asked suspiciously.

"She died in childbirth. They buried the baby in her arms."

Joseph heard the Roman say, "I am sorry." That was what everyone said who heard of his experience, feebly attempting to make his cup less bitter.

"We were happy, because we were together. We combined our two separate lives into a single whole, much like your symbol of the weak separate sticks tied into a bundle that is strong and carried by your lictors, the symbol of Roman power."

"Do you mean that you never quarreled?"

"We had differences and disagreements, but we worked out everything. She was willing to surrender sometimes, and I sometimes. The only time we were unhappy was when we were apart. We grew to depend on each other. She was interested in my thoughts and hopes, more than anyone who ever knew me, with the possible exception of my mother. She expected the best of me, and I tried not to disappoint her."

Julius, leading his stallion by its tether, walked more slowly so that Joseph would not have to talk loud. He did not interrupt.

"Since she has gone, I have found no contentment in life. Everything has lost its enjoyment. No longer does wine taste sweet nor wisteria smell fragrant. Friends have offered me pity, and my mother, advice. I knew that I must leave Cyprus and the painful memories there. My mother tried to get me to remain. Years ago she made a success of her own widowhood by turning all her energies to her small business of dyeing cloth. I offered her money to retire on. She refused, saying she would die if she stopped working. She offered to take me into the business and expand if I would stay. But I knew in the depth of my soul that this was not the answer to my problem. A year before it had been most difficult to break away from her when I got married. I knew if I ever returned to her house that it would become a prison of parental love." Joseph could picture himself withering. "Although it did not make sense at times and still does not, I followed the decision I thought best. I wonder if I'll ever be happy again."

Julius said, "I wonder if I'll ever be happy at all?" Neither spoke again. They headed toward the east, silently wondering what was ahead.

Toward evening they came to a valley that channeled an emaciated river toward the Mediterranean. Dark green trees, rounded like balls, were growing by the stream. The river was a snake of green, slithering through the valley floor of dried grass and plowed fields which were awaiting next season's planting.

The sun was setting as they entered a valley with steep sides. Soon the walls shut out the final lampwick glow of dusk, and the valley was almost dark. They made a circular bend in the road, and everything turned black. The place was cool, and mosquitoes began to buzz about their ears.

38

The Roman's armor clanked as he unbuckled it; then he wrapped up in his wide cloak. Joseph peeled off a blanket from his bundle and used its core with the money in it for his pillow. The valley was as cold as a mountaintop, but he got Julius to agree it was better than the previous night's lodging at the caravanserai. As he grew drowsy, he wondered if something high up the mountainside dislodged a large stone what chances it would have of hitting him. He almost wished one would fall; he was not afraid of dying.

Birds were especially noisy the next morning. Loud chirps annoyed him, and he knew that there would be no sleeping past sunrise. A quick inventory showed that the only food left was some raisins Joseph had wrapped in a napkin before he left Cyprus and tucked in the fold of his garment. They ate all but a handful and began the last leg of their trip to Jerusalem.

The morning, more silent than the previous two days, passed slowly. They used up energy in climbing and perspiring, and they did not choose to lose more in talking. Once they passed through a gorge that had sides which almost met near the top. About noon they finally ascended the ridge and felt a wind blowing from the east. To Joseph the warm air reminded him of the draft from his mother's dye caldrons.

When they looked off to the horizon, they saw a walled city. It was the moment Joseph had dreamed of. The Holy City did not appear hazy, but clear, despite the distance. He could see the dazzling white of the Temple, reflecting the harsh sunshine. It looked as if the buildings were made of mountain-peak snows, carved up and reassembled on the warm foothills by a miracle.

The imperial courier mounted his horse. "I have seen many temples."

Joseph was afraid that the Roman might say something irreverent, and he would have to fight his companion. He wanted this moment alone, peaceful. As quickly as he could, without seeming rude, he said, "You have urgent business in the city; I need to stop and rest. Go ahead, Julius."

Joseph looked in another direction until the soldier was far away. Then he turned to face the Holy City, like a bird charmed by a snake. He fell to his knees to give thanks and to pray for the peace of Jerusalem. Despite his lack of practice, he easily found words for his prayer. He was proud to be a Jew, and he was thankful to be in sight of the Jews' Temple.

Leading the ass nearer the city, Joseph looked down into a great cleared place, a flat courtyard occupying a large section of the crowded town, devoid of houses, but spacious and luxurious. It was the temple area, ornamented with the gleaming building which Herod the Great had erected for the Jews. It was the Temple, God's house, sanctified by location and purpose. It was built, he knew, on the exact spot where Abraham had been willing to offer Isaac. The same spot had been purchased by David for the central shrine of his country and adorned by King Solomon with the first edifice. It had been hallowed by use as the sole sanctuary in a land of many praying people. He moved toward it.

The road carried more traffic now. He passed a shepherd, leading a flock of sheep, and spoke to him. The man replied, "Peace to you. I hope to sell my flock at the sheep market." The contented animals could never guess they were moving toward their slaughter.

As he drew closer, Joseph saw the dark green groves on the Mount of Olives, across the Kidron Valley to the east of the city. He recalled his mother's words, "I want to be buried in Jerusalem at the foot of the Mount of Olives. I do not want to be buried in Cyprus, because my body would have to roll over and over under the ground and under the sea until it got to Jerusalem for the resurrection." Perhaps, he thought, he could buy a burial plot that would satisfy her imaginative hopes.

To the Cypriot, Jerusalem's walls looked forbidding. He said to Olivia, "I feel as David must have felt, when he surveyed the fortified city of the Jebusites and wanted it for his own." Through the slits of the battlements, the sky glowed with a deeper blue.

40

Joseph reached the wall as the sun touched its zenith. Deep shadows between the stones made them stand out separately. Some were smooth. Others were as rough as waves off Cyprus. No two were identical. Together they gave a uniform appearance, not crude, but of time-marked beauty. I hope, Joseph thought, to find something inside.

Shadows underlined the balcony-like adornment above the northwestern gateway, which consisted of a large arch that enveloped a smaller arch within its arms. It was wide enough for two chariots to pass through simultaneously. On an ordinary day, he suspected the place would be deserted at this hour. But the city now had hundreds of pilgrims, each moving about on some errand of importance only to himself. The shepherd, with his flock, had caught up with the curious visitor from Cyprus, and once again shouted, "Peace to you." As Joseph watched him pass through the gate, he estimated it would take four more men of his same size, each standing on the other's shoulders to touch the top of the inner arch.

The trip to Jerusalem was completed, yet incomplete. It had been a tangle of inconvenience and fretful worry. Like a garment unraveling at the edges, it teased him with the prospect of what it was intended to be: the old rabbi might have come to Jerusalem to complete his days in the shadow of the Temple, and the Roman might have expressed an interest in seeking instruction in the Jewish faith. Yet the warp and woof of the trip irritated his mind with memories of sullen sailors, a hesitant ship, a tiresome walk, heat, mosquitoes, vermin, and for traveling companions a garrulous old man, a donkey, and a Gentile. Still, he recalled, feeling guilty, the companions had contributed to the only enjoyable part of the journey. His only happy recollections centered on his two fellow travelers—the rabbi and the soldier, as diverse as Cain and Abel, yet both dearer to him after their departure than the gold he had hidden in his baggage. Joseph entered the gate, preoccupied with a desire to see again his rabbi and his Roman friend, and forgot to pray the pilgrim's prayer of rejoicing. He never guessed that the next few hours would change the entire course of his life.

III.

Like ingredients in a raisin-almond cake, the holiday populace was stirred and mixed into a strange conglomeration. Joseph felt squeezed and kneaded by the pressures of the compact city. He noticed the houses of Jerusalem clinging together, dovetailing and overlapping, leaving almost no space for movement or transportation. He saw streets so narrow that two fully-loaded donkeys could scarcely pass each other. Nowhere was the mixing and squeezing together of people more evident than on the bridge that led from the western ridge of the Holy City, across the Tyropoeon Valley, to the sacred area of the Temple. On that magnificent royal structure, supported by soaring arches of stone, he spied a familiar figure. The crowd slowed down. Just ahead, impeding the progress, was a large man shuffling along. Joseph wondered how it could be his rabbi and reached out for his sleeve.

A strange voice said, "You want to take something from me?"

"No, you look like someone I know. I'd like to help you."

"Normal people don't talk like that. You must be one of those Nazarenes. Leave me alone."

Puzzled, Joseph looked around. Something about the crowds moving across the bridge frightened him. They reminded him of a herd of cattle, restless when a distant thunderstorm approaches. He saw, at that moment, only one other animal besides his own, another donkey, balancing two big cages filled with fluttering, white doves. Everyone in the crowd of people, smelling of onions and sweat, seemed determined to push his way ahead, going or returning.

Like a blind man, Joseph groped his way over to the edge of the drifting crowd and stopped near the bridge rail with its stone coping. A workman, carrying one end of a heavy beam, cursed at him for stopping. Preoccupied Joseph paid no attention to the carrier, for he knew if he did not stop moving, he would soon be inside the walls of the sacred area, too close to see the lovely panorama that he hungered to study. He wanted to look at the Temple from the middle of the bridge, regardless of the impatient throng. He coaxed his donkey as close to the rail as possible, so as not to impede the flow of the human river.

"The wind has changed. It is coming from the desert." A man about his same age was speaking to a wrinkled traveling companion, who used a walking stick. Joseph overheard him say, "This east wind will likely bring hot weather for the next three days."

Joseph did not notice the heat but he smelled a nauseating odor. Then he realized that the unaccustomed east wind was blowing smells from the great altar of burnt offering toward the city. Even here on the bridge, the horrible reek of burning animal flesh tempted him to run in the other direction and to forget about his visit to the hallowed place. The revolting stench, intensified by the additional pungency of incense, made him bury his nose in the sleeve of his cloak.

Eventually, when he had grown accustomed to the odor, he again looked toward the marvels of Mount Moriah. He noted the milk-colored stone wall that outlined the entire sacred area. It was as high as many cities boasted for their outside walls of protection. Beyond these rose thin inner walls that enclosed the area restricted to Jews alone. Above these projected the tall, straight sides of the Temple itself. The magnificent building was partly overlaid with gold. Other unadorned parts revealed stones as white as Mount Hermon's snow. On the roof were golden spikes to keep birds from defiling it. The sight, even here from the west, toward the rear of the Temple, was the most beautiful he had ever seen. He had heard his mother speak of the view from the Mount of Olives toward the front of the Temple, but he wondered how that view could be any lovelier.

Like seeds planted long ago and beginning to germinate after a long-awaited rain, songs from the psalter sprouted from his weary mind. "I was glad when they said unto me, Let us go into the house of the Lord."

"Blessed is the man whom thou choosest, and causest to ap-

43

proach unto thee, that he may dwell in thy courts: we shall be satisfied with the goodness of thy house, even of thy holy temple."

The longer he looked, the more something disturbed his appreciative view. Like a fly on a honey cake, the large building at the northwest corner of the Temple walls seemed to draw away the focus of his attention. It was solid and sturdy, like a fortress, with towers at each of the corners—yet the tower nearest the Temple area was extraordinarily high. To a stranger he said, "What building is that?" As he pointed, two workmen carrying stones attached by ropes to poles bumped into his arm.

The man he questioned said abruptly, "Why ask me? I'm a visitor, too." He walked off leaving Joseph unanswered.

Joseph spotted a middle-aged man, moving more slowly, accompanied by a woman with a black shawl over her head. He looked more approachable, and Joseph asked him about the curious tower, just beyond the Temple wall.

"That," he paused for a sigh of resignation, "is the Fortress Antonia." The helpful stranger was eating grapes from a glistening full cluster. He offered them neither to the silent woman accompanying him nor to Joseph, who had not eaten since early morning. The more grapes the man ate, the hungrier Joseph became. The man held the bunch in front of his mouth and then protruded his lips to pull off the grapes, one by one. He continued to nibble, as he spoke. "Herod the Great is responsibile for the way it looks and for its name. He was a shrewd politician and named it for Mark Antony, who then seemed on his way to dominating the entire Roman Empire. Herod had that tallest tower built on the southeast corner so he, himself, could look over into the Temple area and see what was going on. He was always suspicious. Herod died while I was still a small child, and I never got to see him. But I have heard of the terrible things he did to his enemies and even to members of his own family."

Joseph wished that this stranger were as generous with his grapes as with his words. "The fortress with its turrets detracts from the beauty of the Temple."

The stranger spit some seeds over the bridge into the valley.

"That building is a symbol of outsiders attempting to dominate all of our life, even our religious life. A Roman cohort is quartered there now. They can look down on our people in the sacred place and laugh at our customs." His eyelids lifted and his eyes bulged. "But they can never enter the Temple. They can never pull it down. One day God will drive them out of our land."

Joseph sensed that the man would be willing to spend the afternoon there on the busy bridge, reciting the history of the Jews and denouncing their oppressors. "Thank you, my father," he said appreciatively and moved on. He remembered the handful of raisins he had hidden inside a napkin tied to his belt. He munched on them as he neared the gateway.

As he completed crossing the bridge, he noted the outside walls of large ashlar blocks, nine to fifteen feet long and three to four feet high. The stones were dressed around their margins with a smooth area from two to four inches wide. Joseph knew that an uncalculated amount of labor had gone into the structure.

He entered a double-arched gate and momentarily left the bright sunlight to feel a cool caress from the shade. Huddled along the walls on both sides of this gate and in between the columns that supported the middle were pitiful beggars. Crouching there in the shade were people with drawn, gaunt faces, looking more like skeletons than living people. Most of them were men, but two were women with wild, touseled hair. A few held out bony hands for alms, but many extended begging bowls. Joseph paused and reached into his robe. He pulled out some tiny coins and went to each beggar to give him one. With pleading eyes, each one stared at him and mumbled his thanks.

He was about to pass inside to the courtyard, when the last beggar diverted his eyes and expressed no thanks. Impulsively, Joseph asked, "Can you say nothing?" Looking at the man again he said, "Didn't I know you on Cyprus?" A simple denial would have been sufficient, but the poor wretch pulled a shawl over his head. Joseph did not get a good enough look to tell for sure, but he thought the man resembled the synagogue cantor who had gone to Jerusalem to study and was still receiving regular gifts from the

45

Cypriot congregation. Under the shawl, the man coughed and coughed until Joseph left.

Large groups of people stood inside porticos formed by Corinthian columns of the courtyard and discussed matters of importance. The only people in the open courtyard were either heading for or coming from a place of shade. In that magnificent place, Olivia, his dusty little donkey, seemed inappropriate. Joseph had noticed one or two animals tied at the gateway near the beggars, but none was as packed with clothing and valuables as Olivia. Like a coincidental answer to a holy man's prayer, a boy came forward to ask something. The child's hair might have been black, but it looked the color of smoke because it was so full of dust. "Want me to watch your donkey while you visit the Temple?"

"Why, yes," said the surprised traveler. They were the first words spoken to him in this sanctified city that seemed to show a real interest in himself as a person. They made him think of Rufus. The words had come from a simple child, and he thought, "A little child shall lead them."

Abruptly, the boy punctured the holy illusion. "It will cost you four mites—in advance."

Any other time, Joseph would have chuckled over the clever enterprise of such a child. Yet, today, everything seemed so oppressively serious that he did not laugh; he was too exhausted to get angry. Instead, he gave up to a resignation of disappointment and handed the boy the coins and the ass's reins. "What's your name?"

Just then, two priests in white linen robes and turbans passed by—colorless except for belts embroidered in blue, purple, and scarlet. In front of them marched two Levites, in simple white robes. Joseph looked at these assistants with some degree of pity, for he knew from his father what their life was like.

The lad shouted his name, "Jacob," and disappeared.

In the holy crowd, he did not know one person, and none called him by name. He was alone. Although it was afternoon, he began to feel a midnight of despair. He wondered if he had come all this distance just to look at stone walls and Corinthian columns.

Then he moved toward a group of sweating workers, who were busy placing the beams he had seen being transported across the bridge. They were attaching the highly-polished wooden members to project into the courtyard, and then they were nailing colorful pieces of awning to them. He watched as one booth was completed, and an official looking group of men moved in a table and chairs and began to stack coins for exchange. He said to one, "Am I correct in thinking I can't drop a coin like this into the treasury?" He held up the last coin in his possession; it was a denarius bearing a sculptured portrait of Tiberius Caesar.

"Indeed, not!" came the haughty answer. "Do you not know that such a coin, bearing an image, is forbidden? Here, I will change it for a Judean coin."

He accepted the coin, minted some one hundred years earlier and worth much less. But Joseph thought, Giving a coin to the Temple treasury might lift my spirits.

As Joseph headed across the paved area of the Court of the Gentiles, he realized that the sacred area was not a perfect square as his rabbi had taught. At the balustrade that separates the Jewish area from the Court of the Gentiles, he noticed a Greek slave resting on the barrier, studying the inner court, with its walls and steps. Joseph went up the steps inside the high walls of the inner court and entered by the Beautiful Gate, with doors of Corinthian bronze. Around the wall in the Court of Women there were several containers, which looked like cooking vessels that might supply soup to a company of soldiers. Some were labeled shekel dues, bird offerings, wood offerings, frankincense, gold for the mercy seat; six unmarked containers were for freewill offerings. Joseph went to one of the latter and dropped in the ancient Judean coin. It made a lovely, hollow sound. He had no more spending money left—only the treasure from his land.

Expectantly Joseph mounted the long flight of steps that leads from the Court of the Women to the Court of Israel. Some mystic urge had driven him to this section, devoted exclusively to the use

47

of Hebrew men.

It seemed, at first, like the other courts, except less colorful. Then he realized that with the lack of Roman-clothed Gentiles and Jewish women, the Court of Israel held only elders in dark cloaks and drab tunics.

He observed various compartments that opened on to the court. They were similar to the booths of the Gentile court, yet these were of permanent stone construction. They were like lecture rooms he remembered at the Academy of Salamis, with sides almost completely opened for light and breezes.

From one of these came the high, shrill voice of a person either in great pain or intense anger. He heard these words: "And the preparation is just as important as the sabbath. You must build a fence around the preparation to hold out the thieves who would steal the sabbath." As he arrived on the threshold, Joseph learned that the voice came from a scrawny little man who resembled a bird he had once seen, a black-feathered one that imitated human speech.

Then the mellow voice of an older man began to dominate the group. "The sabbath was given for itself and by itself; we must not try to make an additional sabbath out of the eve of the sabbath."

Joseph stepped inside the alcove and sat on the floor with some of the younger men. Two of them turned to stare at him, but no one said a word. He knew that it was his privilege to visit this discussion of the law if he desired.

The birdman spoke again. "The sages say, 'A tailor should not go out with a needle stuck in his garment on the eve of the sabbath.' "

One of the younger men seated on the floor said, "Why is there a restriction against wearing the needle, since he does not carry it like a burden?"

Joseph noticed a table in the far corner of the room, where a scribe was taking down both questions and answers.

Exasperated, the man with the shrill voice spoke again, his long stringy neck was vibrating like a plucked lyre. "Do you not see that the needle is the sign of his trade, just as the carpenter carries a chip of wood behind his ear and the dyer a color sample around his neck? When people see these symbols of the trade on the eve of the sabbath, they will recognize the artisan and likely employ him for a task that cannot be completed before the sabbath commences."

Words of approval came from an elderly man, seated near the front of the room in the only comfortable looking chair there. He had a white beard that cascaded from his face like a turbulent waterfall. He bewailed people who desecrate the sabbath because of false claims. Then he summarized his views in a boiled-down statement: "If one kills vermin on the sabbath, it is as though he killed a camel."

The man who looked and sounded like a bird, elated to have such venerable support, spoke again. "Our rabbis taught this: 'If one searches his garments on the sabbath, he may press the vermin and throw it away, providing that he does not kill it.' These are worthy words that we of the House of Shemmai know well and honor. We could not expect the House of Hillel to understand their worth."

Others in the alcove began to murmur in disagreement. Joseph did not care to hear a religious debate between two disagreeing factions. He moved to the door and crouched so as not to call undue attention to his departure. As he went out, someone was questioning the House of Shemmai about whether or not a woman's earrings were forbidden burdens to be born on the sabbath.

Joseph felt sorry for these pathetic men, arguing about the trivialities of the law. This punctilious dogmatism contrasted with his memories of his mother's view of the seventh day. She always called it "a joy of the soul." She always looked forward to the end of the week, when she would lay aside her cooking garment, put down her broom, and light the sabbath lamp, serene and happy. She observed the day and taught her family to revere it as one of happiness and holiness. Certainly, she taught her children basic rules about the sabbath, but always she explained that these were made out of love to set it apart from other days. Even she had occasionally violated the stricter rules and quoted, "When an ox

49

falls into a ditch on the sabbath, it must be saved." Her observance was spontaneous, neither legalistic nor mechanical.

The contrast disgusted Joseph, so he looked for something to divert his mind. He regretted that he had anticipated an esoteric experience from the Temple. It had not turned out to be the holy atmosphere he had expected to breathe. There was nothing more in the Court of Israel to interest him, but he paused in the central entranceway, straining his eyes for a view of the Court of the Priests and beyond. He glimpsed for the first time the great smoking altar of burnt offering that continued to emit a horrible odor. He could easily imagine the sacred butchery of the sacrifice, with the reek of animals just disemboweled. Behind the altar he saw the Temple itself. Through the high opening of the vestibule, he could make out the faintly visible and utterly unbelievable golden vine with its clusters of grapes as tall as a man. The sight made him recall the frequent Roman taunt that Jews worship Bacchus, the god of wine, after all. In the doorway, he saw the curtain of Babylonian tapestry, embroidered with a motif of sun, moon, and stars—God's universe.

Just as he was about to forget his loneliness in the marvels of the Temple, he heard loud voices beyond the wall. They were hurried and sharp, with hints of intended violence. Then a runner came through the doorway and screamed for the entire courtyard to hear, "They caught a *goy.*"

The words were like a fire alarm. Everyone began moving toward the Court of the Gentiles. The classroom he had just attended emptied itself in haste. The oldest man with the gray beard who had used the comfortable chair was now running, lifting the skirts of his garment up to his ancient knees.

Excitedly Joseph asked, "What is the commotion?" No one stopped to answer him. All were drawn by the tide of curiosity and the undercurrent of hate. Everyone, including Joseph, was pulled toward the vortex of the human whirlpool. They passed the Court of Women and headed for the balustrade of the lower court.

It was late afternoon and tempers were on edge. People had been goaded, teased, and irritated by the warm desert wind. A man on the edge of the gathered crowd turned back to look at the group coming from the Court of Israel. He had a beard the color of washed copper. He looked directly at Joseph and said, "We have caught a Greek slave about to break a law."

Joseph looked at the nearest opening of the balustrade and saw lounging in it a Greek slave, desperately trying to look unconcerned. He was surrounded by angry Jews, whose demanding faces were almost touching his. He heard the Greek talking in a loud but quavering voice, "Of course, I can read the warning. It says, 'Let no one of the Gentiles enter inside the barrier around the sanctuary and the porch; and if he transgresses he shall bear the blame for his ensuing death.' "

A large man, with a bullish neck, grabbed the slave as if he were a wild ass in an open field. Panting heavily, the big man said, "He knows what he has done."

The frightened slave said, "I was standing in the doorway. I was just curious to find out more about your religion."

The bullish man gasped, "We are not concerned about his purpose for doing this terrible thing. He took a step past the threshold, conscious of the law."

Like a pack of dogs sniffing fresh meat, the people waited silent and not moving. Joseph pushed into the sullen crowd and shouted to the puffing orator. "Why do you not turn him over to the Romans?"

People in the pack yelled, "No, no, no." They continued the short, repetitive blasts, and ones near Joseph glared at him.

The man with the copper beard said to him, "They are ready for blood. Their fury is worse during the Holy Days. They are frustrated politically and religiously. They despise the Romans and have few ways of releasing their hostility except in religious scrupulosity."

The big man said to the mob, "If we turn him over to the Romans, they will withhold judgment. If we transact our own penalty, then they can do nothing." He panted and grinned. "They cannot punish all of us." People in the mad throng began to cheer, as if they were attending a gladiatorial event.

"Hurry," someone urged.

"Let us carry out justice," the leader shouted. The mob, like a herd of sweating, puffing, enraged animals began moving toward the Beautiful Gate, half pushing and pulling the victim.

Joseph impetuously cried to them, "Wait. Take me instead. Let him go. Punish me." He did not know what spirit possessed him to speak the words. They seemed to come from beyond himself. But the inexplicable words were unheeded. The savages went off, leaving only the most venerable and weakest elders behind.

The court was almost completely deserted. It was now quiet enough for worship, but Joseph did not feel reverent. He had heard that people could be led like sheep. He had been told that religious people could act most irreligiously. He now knew what it was to see an angry bigot fan the emotional sparks of a crowd into a conflagration. He had always desired to see this for himself. Now that he had witnessed the sickening transformation, he was disgusted. For him it had been a senseless orgy—a pack of wolves attacking a wounded doe.

In the quiet of the late afternoon, he was startled by the triple blast of trumpets, ironically calling for silence at the appointed time for prayer.

Joseph dragged his feet over the marble pavement of the Court of Gentiles, away from the silvery fanfare. His throat seemed filled with warm salty water, and his stomach felt as if it had started digesting itself. He felt as he used to when, as a child, he was forced to eat cooked greens and boiled eggplant. After he forced them down, they always came back up. Now, becoming worried over the spectacle of an illness in the hallowed court, he recalled the word of a rabbi, "One must not cause himself to vomit in the street, out of decency." Yet he answered that thought with the view that his sickness was not self-induced but irresistible. His active mind was like the discussion he had just left. He could think of questions, of answers, of counter-questions, of refutations, of authorities, and of related incidents. Dizzy and nauseated, he stumbled through the Court of the Women and down across the Court of the Gentiles. He went to the corner of the ambulatory, where the southern and eastern walls converged high above the Kidron Valley. He judged that it must be one hundred eighty to two hundred feet to the bottom. He coughed up the few raisins that were in his stomach, undigested. They fell only a few feet into some bushes growing from the rocks. Then he retched unproductively several times.

At that moment he wished for his mother to place a cold cloth on his head, as she had done when he was a youth. Even though she had objected to his going to the gymnasium and participating in the races, she always nursed him when he returned home, tired out, and sometimes nauseated.

With his vision blurred and his head swaying, Joseph tried to look down the Kidron Valley in the direction of the Valley of Hinnon, which Jews had abhorred because of human sacrifices once offered there. It was now used as a dump. Then he tried to look across the valley to the Mount of Offence, where Solomon had built pagan altars for his wives. Everything appeared as hazy as a reflection in a polished metal mirror.

When Joseph looked down, his vision cleared. The precipice allured him. It dazzled and mystified him. It performed a Salome-dance before his imagination that made him promise anything. His chest yearned for the rocks below. He said, half aloud, "My life is worth no more than a melon."

He thought of the beautifully arched fall of a melon, as it might whoosh through the air on a flight downward. The moments would stretch out and lengthen as it fell, the distance transforming the journey into a feather-glide of happiness.

Joseph lifted himself to the parapet and felt a warm blast of air. He looked at the pointed top of a cypress that began far down the mountainside growing and stretching upward, even with him as he tottered on the ledge.

Joseph's thoughts returned to the floating melon. It would ultimately reach the bottom and embrace the rocks as they jumped upward to meet it, splitting into thousands of morsels for industrious ants to carry away.

He wobbled a little. The green below looked refreshing. He no longer smelled the horrible reek from the altar of burnt offering.

53

His hand stopped trembling, and the dizzy swaying of his head also stopped. He wondered if anyone would find his body, or if the vultures would take away the fragments to their lairs. Suddenly, he remembered his money. Those sculptured coins of gold, a sacred trust, instantly sobered him. The memory caused him to begin trembling again. The money from his father's inheritance would be thrown away, discarded. Since he could not pass along his father's name to children of his own, he must, at least, use the money wisely, as a memorial to the deceased Levite.

He could kill himself later, but the money must be looked after now. He wondered if this thought came from cowardice or from real concern. Suddenly, he stepped back on the pavement of the portico, glad to be alive, actually happy that he had not made the foolish plunge.

At that instant, Joseph felt a tug on his coat sleeve. The frightened Jacob said, "Your donkey has disappeared."

Joseph, controlling his fury, asked, "Did you see which direction she went in?"

"No," replied the truthful lad, "I was talking to my friend, the flute salesman. Perhaps an evil spirit possessed her and made her invisible."

"Lazy fool. Say nothing to me about spirits. Come and help me look for her."

They started across the royal bridge, which was not as crowded now. When he came to the spot where he had stopped to admire the Temple walls, Joseph saw his Olivia waiting peacefully by the far approach to the bridge. Afraid that the donkey might bolt and run, he dashed toward her. Suddenly, he caught a glimpse of two men bearing a wooden beam, which quickly expanded to gigantic size and excluded anything else from his vision. He felt his knees dissolving like melting butter, and his head became as uncontrollable as a bridegroom drunk on new wine. For some strange reason, he knew that he was lying motionless on the stone passageway, and he felt something warm and sticky on his forehead and at the back of his neck.

IV.

Joseph tried to subdue his wild thoughts and discover where he was. Then he thought he knew. He was swimming under water, with pressure pounding in his ears and tiring his lungs; he tried to rise to the surface. He could almost see his wife and the rabbi through fathoms of water, but the surface distorted their faces and made them look like other people. As she stood over the water's edge, her face looked younger. The rabbi, too, looked younger. He saw them look at each other and converse, although he could hear nothing but the humming of moving water.

It seemed to Joseph that he was swimming in the green crystal waters off the seawall at Caesarea. He was searching for something along the sandy bottom. The pressure pushed his skull harder, and the light in the water turned murky in a twilight of pain.

Joseph sensed that something strange was happening. However, the lovely face looking down into his could be only his wife's; yet it did not look like her. With the fear that she had changed faces without telling him, he felt himself again sinking to the bottom.

There was no way for Joseph to tell time, no stars above his head, no sun in the sky. Yet he had the impression that time was passing, not slowly as on the boat trip, but quickly as in his frantic dash for the lost donkey. Then he suddenly said aloud, "I must stop Olivia. That donkey is borrowed." But he felt firm arms pushing back his shoulders.

He heard a mellow voice. "We have your donkey. She is well taken care of." The words, from some undetermined origin, were like a sleeping potion. They caused him to lie back on his cot and relax. Other words became a mumble of distant drums in his drowsy ears.

Everything was dark in Joseph's world as he felt his head being raised. Somewhere in the room a lamp was flickering, but he could not see it—all he could see were restless shadows. Some power

55

outside himself held a bowl of soup to his lips, and an angelic voice said, "Please, drink this." He was puzzled that it was so hard for him to obey. Some of the warm broth dripped off his chin, but he felt a tiny amount slide down his throat. Food dripping, lamp flickering, shadows darting—everything seemed to be moving.

He moved, slipping and falling over the courtyard of the Temple; Joseph believed that he was again being driven toward the dangerous south-east corner called "the pinnacle." He seemed to be throwing away pieces of gold as he rolled faster toward the wall. He felt like a dried leaf in the wintry wind, incapable of directing its course, completely at the mercy of the overpowering blast. He must stop. He tried to surpass the wind's noise with a moan. Then, as he stood for a brief moment on the parapet of the Temple wall, looking down into the Kidron Valley, he knew that he did not want to die. Frantic that some force might push him, he yelled, "No! No!"

A quiet voice answered. "Everything is all right, my brother." His brow felt the touch of a hand.

Instead of falling, he drifted into a haze of memories: his boyhood home at Cyprus, his mother kindling the sabbath light, his wrestling at the gymnasium, his friends listening to his oration at the academy, and his participation in synagogue services. The return of these ancient memories, now vivid and thrilling, further mystified him. The impossible was occurring, and it seemed that the river of time was flowing backwards.

Joseph awakened. He realized that he had been trying to wake up for a long time. Now he opened his eyes and saw a stranger who looked friendly. An older man with the longest nose he had ever seen was sitting by his bed. Joseph greeted him, "Shalom."

The word was a tiny spark that lighted a flame of pleasant associations of good health, prosperity, and freedom from enmity.

The man responded strangely, as if he had been given a valuable present. He exclaimed, "Praise be to the Lord." Then he knocked over his stool as he rushed to the door of the room. "Sarah, come quickly."

The man returned, and Joseph smiled at him. A great toothy

56

grin made the man's nose seem even longer and multiplied tiny lines around his eyes. Despite the wrinkles and the odd nose, his face was pleasant.

A young girl rushed to the bedside, with her robe billowing like the wings of a flying bird. "Is he . . . all right?"

"How long," asked Joseph, "have I been asleep?"

The man, who introduced himself as Zadok, said, "This is the tenth day of Tishri."

"The Day of Atonement," Joseph gasped.

"Yes, you came to us on the third day of the month."

Sarah added, "You have been very sick since then."

Zadok said, "Your recovery is largely due to this dear girl's care."

Modestly, she said, "I did very little." When she looked down, Joseph noticed her fair skin. Her complexion was light—not the pallor of aristocratic women who avoid the sun—but a delicate sea shell shade. Her eyelashes were long and black. Her lips were as lovely as the scrolls of the law. Admiring her loveliness brought back to his mind the delirious visions of his wife. Now he understood; it was this young girl, Sarah, who had stood above his bed and resembled his lost mate as she seemed to search the waters with her eyes.

The host said, "She is my granddaughter and lives here to cook for me. She made a different soup or broth for you each day. While you were asleep, it was very difficult to get you to drink it. But she had patience, and we were able to get a little nourishment into you each day."

"I am as grateful as a drowning man, pulled from the waves." Joseph knew that his voice was weak and high-pitched. "How did you find me?"

"The lad brought you to us. You see, I am a potter."

"What kind?"

"I make clay lamps for a living. The boy, Jacob, comes by to watch me. He will become my apprentice when he grows a little older." Zadok smiled at his granddaughter, and Joseph felt a contentment he had not known for many months. It was difficult for

57

him to concentrate on the old man's explanation. "The boy could not take you to his own place. There are several children, and they all live together in a tiny house with their grandmother."

"It was Zadok's haste that saved your life, and do not let him tell you otherwise."

The potter continued. "I merely did what was needed at the moment. The boy came running to my place. You will see that we are located near the bridge. I am surrounded here by cheesemakers, but I prefer this location near the Temple to the Street of the Potters. I was just taking my merchandise into the house for the evening, when Jacob came running up saying a stranger was hurt on the head and bleeding. He was very worried, claiming it was all his fault."

Joseph recalled the boy's bargain to watch his animal. "Jacob is a clever boy."

"He thinks ahead, more like a man than a child. Well, to continue, I grabbed a wet cloth and a dry one. When I got to you, I had to push through the crowd. No one was doing anything—all were just standing and looking. As soon as I put the cool, wet cloth to your wounds, they began to stop bleeding. Then I tied up your head and got three other men to help me bring you here. The donkey is tied out back with my goat."

Joseph said, "I can never repay your kindness. I want you, Sarah, and the boy to take half my possessions." Joseph knew that he was in the presence of energetic, honest people, who had to work six days a week to keep from starving. He honestly wanted them to take half his coins. He also knew that few people ever return to the land of the living after going as close as he had gone to the river of death. Even in his bruised brain, he knew that the kind old man had cared for his body's needs as if he had been watching over a baby, snatched from its mother, dependent and helpless. The man had been willing to soil his hands to care for this stranger.

Sarah responded, straightening her posture. "We accept your thanks, but we cannot accept your offer."

Zadok echoed her impulsive answer and added, "We are doing for you only what we have been commanded."

58

Exhausted by the brief conversation, Joseph let his eyelids relax. They closed out the world of the present and opened the windows of dreamy memories. Grateful to have recovered on this sacred day of fasting and prayer, he found his mind too fatigued to put his feelings into actual words of a prayer. Like a worked-out copper mine, he felt that he had nothing left to offer the Lord; but he was grateful to be alive. He was not asleep, but he rested the remainder of the afternoon.

Zadok sent Sarah outside several times to see if the sun had set. When she assured him that the day was over, he took food. "This Day of Atonement has been a day of nourishment for my soul. I am thankful to our Savior for the answered prayer."

From his cot, Joseph asked the man at the table, "What do you mean?"

"I prayed to our Messiah for your health. He is the Great Physician, and he answered."

Joseph's head was hurting too much for him to ask more about the references to Messiah and Savior. He recalled another reference that day which piqued his curiosity. When they were discussing his weakened condition, Joseph had asked, "Should I eat anything on this fast day?"

Zadok had answered, "Yes, my friend. You need all the strength you can get. The Creator knows your physical needs as well as your spiritual condition. He knows that you can pray a repentant prayer, even with a full meal in your stomach. I, myself, have fasted today. However, I must confess that I have wondered about it. I believe that the Messiah has made the perfect sacrifice. And if this is true, a sinner's fasting or a high priest's releasing a scapegoat can make little difference."

Joseph's mind, almost as tired as his body, could not comprehend and floated back to the tangle of memories and dreams.

Joseph woke up early. Only the slightest change from black to gray had occurred in the portion of the sky that showed through his window. He was rested, and pushed on his elbows to get up. He was able to make that much progress with no effort. Then he threw back the covers and put his feet on the floor. He stood up

59

right but felt like a fox that had glutted itself in a ripe vineyard. His head was too dizzy to allow him to take even one step from his bed.

Resigned to his fate, he lay back on the cot, slowly recovering from the dizzy attack. Knowing that his physical activities would have to be limited for awhile longer, Joseph decided to exercise his mind.

He rehearsed the story of his rescue and convalescence in this place, the small front room of the potter's house. Joseph's cot had been moved into this room for his privacy. Sarah, Zadok, and Joseph each had a separate room. When he had satisfied his curiosity about location, he then turned to time. This dawn was like any number of sunrises, during the spring, summer, or fall. He knew only that it was not the rainy season, but he had to work his mind to plow up the date. Then he cultivated his memory of the wonderful month of Tishri that is noted for its quick succession of holy days. On the first is the New Year's celebration. On the tenth is the Day of Atonement. On the fifteenth begins the Feast of Booths which lasts eight days. In between the tenth and fifteen was the period in which Joseph had hoped to return to Caesarea to check on his old friend and to return the donkey.

Such a journey was now out of the question. Joseph knew that it would take days to regain his strength. He knew that it might be several weeks before he would be able to travel. He heard someone going out to the courtyard to milk the goat.

On this eleventh morning of Tishri, Zadok brought warm goat milk and said, "I did not work on 'the day,' so I must go for a fresh supply of clay today. Sarah will be here, if you need anything."

Joseph, who had trouble remembering their names, said farewell to this new friend, and then he began to stare at Sarah. Sitting by an open window, she was working on an old garment, applying a patch very carefully so that it would not be noticeable. Her face was as lovely as any he had seen in Salamis or Caesarea.

As he studied her beauty, Joseph rubbed his chin. He was surprised to feel a rough growth of beard. Never before had he allowed

60

his face to be covered with a beard; he had always kept it clean shaven in the Roman fashion. Now he became concerned about how he might look to his nurse.

She interrupted his apology. "I like a beard. It makes me think of the prophets of old times." Although her chair was facing his cot, she did not look up. She continued her mending.

Joseph disliked silence as much as he disliked bragging people. Suddenly he asked, "How old are you?" He realized how rude and impertinent his question might sound, but it was too late.

Without hesitation, she said, "Eighteen years."

Joseph tried not to show surprise. He thought that she looked younger than eighteen. Knowing that most girls were married by this age, he expected her to become defensive and embarrassed. She continued to work. Although he enjoyed being in the same room with her, he found it much more difficult to carry on a conversation with her than with the Roman soldier. She responded to his questions, but she did not ask him anything or bring up any new topics.

A knock at the door caused both Joseph and Sarah to jump. Without waiting to be admitted, Jacob, who had kept his donkey, came into the room to see how the patient was doing. Sarah explained, "He has been coming every day."

The boy smiled toward the floor. "I brought you a flute." Jacob shifted his weight from one bare foot to the other and finally left.

When Zadok returned, Joseph enjoyed telling him the events of the day, especially about the boy's visit. Then he asked, "Aren't you pleased with my progress?"

"Very much," he answered. Then he looked toward Sarah and said, "A physician I talked with told me that we should have been feeding him gall of fish for medicinal purposes. Perhaps he would have recovered more quickly."

"Don't worry, my friend, I don't believe the fish gall would have speeded my recovery one jot. Even if I had been taken to the house of that physician, I doubt that he could have saved my life. I am very pleased with the recovery I owe to you and to Sarah."

"And to the Messiah," she added.

That night, as Joseph lay resting, tired from a full day of con-

61

sciousness, he saw a stranger come through the door and introduce himself to Zadok. Since the man was fingering a cylindrical pottery container, he supposed that it was a regular business call. He did not listen to the conversation, at first, but studied the thin young stranger, who constantly pushed back a shock of black hair that fell over his forehead. Either his eyes were more protruded than most people's or else his thin face made them appear so. Zadok tried to get him to sit on one of the stools at the table. Refusing, he spoke in frenzied spurts. "You look like a true Son of David. You will need one of these." He removed the cover from the pottery jar, the kind which some people put valuable documents into for safe burial. What he brought out was not a document but a dagger. It had a sharp point and in the lamplight seemed to have no evidence of rust. Zadok moved his lips together in a chewing manner and looked uncomprehending as his lips smacked meaninglessly.

The impatient young man said, "We are providing these at no profit. My friends and I charge only what they cost us."

"Friend, you have come to the wrong house."

"No, every house is right. Every man must arm himself for Zion's coming war. If only one half the Jews would use daggers, we could kill every Roman on our soil tonight."

Zadok said, "No, that's not the way. Such an action might remove the soldiers for a short while. But Rome would send replacements, perhaps harsh mercenaries from beyond the Danube. These troops could slaughter our entire race."

"Not if we are ready for them."

"The Nazarene has brought peace to our hearts, and he said that ones who take the sword will . . ."

"He was a foolish dreamer. I knew two older men who followed him." The stranger pushed back his stubborn hair as he recalled their names. "Simon the Zealot and Judas Iscariot."

"I know Simon, but I never knew Judas."

The dagger man answered, "He died disappointed—fooled by the Galilean who promised a new kingdom."

"He was not fooled; he deliberately misunderstood. My brother,

62

don't make a mistake just as tragic. Come and study the words of the Messiah."

"Enough of this foolishness. I must go to other houses. I can find brave men with clear minds elsewhere."

As the door slammed, Joseph heard Zadok say, "Shalom." He doubted that the incendiary youth had heard.

Others, besides this insurrectionist came to the door. A few neighbors brought strong smelling cheeses and pottage. Some came for no other purpose, he guessed, but to stare at the stranger with the bandaged head. Many children came in for brief moments. Sarah said that she could keep them out, but Joseph told her he did not mind their brief visits.

The next few days rushed past in a succession of new accomplishments for the convalescing Joseph. A few steps from the bed twice a day, then a trip to the table to eat, next short walks out to the courtyard to see Olivia, and finally the big journey out the front door and into the street.

What he saw there surprised him: in between this door and the door to the workroom was a display of merchandise. Laid out neatly on shelves, built like stairsteps, and also on the ground, were scores of pottery lamps. All were alike, and Joseph wondered why Zadok, the potter, did not display just one lamp as a sample and sell others from it.

Zadok must have guessed his thoughts. "A large display attracts customers."

Joseph leaned against the side of the doorpost and listened to a customer try to bargain with the man. This simple, straightforward potter set one price, as low as possible, and stuck with it, despite threats of going to a competitor or pleadings of poverty. Joseph was enthralled to hear a new widow, forgetting her moans and wails for a few moments, try to get Zadok to lower the price of a new lamp to be placed in her husband's tomb. The potter was kind but firm.

As soreness and pain left his body, so did feelings of loneliness and searching. He did not bother to solve any deep riddles of life and death but lived day by day, watching the craft of his host.

Zadok had placed his potter's wheel just inside the door to his workroom. He could watch his street display from that vantage point, and if a customer came up, he could leave the unfinished work for a few minutes in order to make a sale. He sat down and started pumping with his foot. The lump of cool, moist clay began to rotate slowly, then spin. Zadok wet his hands, and they glided over the pliant mass with a lover's caress.

Next the potter deftly inserted his index finger into the clay. His hands were caked with various layers of drying clay and looked like a lizard's skin. Then he curved his buff-colored finger and flattened the spinning lamp at the same time. He made it resemble a small bowl, and Joseph realized that this would become the oil reservoir. The mud-spattered Zadok continued to flatten the container until it suited him; the spectator judged that it was almost as broad as his palm and as high as the width of his thumb. Joseph asked, "Do you make any measurements or use a model?" He learned that the potter made no measurements, for the practice of years had produced speed and certainty in his craft. In a final whirl of speed, he shaped a flange around the filling hole and allowed the wheel to coast to a stop.

Zadok took the bowl from the wheel and handed it to his guest, who handled it as a bachelor holds a baby. "You won't hurt it," the older man said. "But this is not yet a lamp. It must have a nozzle."

Joseph watched Zadok reach into a container that was covered by a wet cloth. He took out a nozzle that previously had been shaped with a knife from pliable clay. With dexterity, the crafts-man attached the nozzle, picked up a punch and with it made a hole into the reservoir, and then with his knife he smoothed the juncture of the nozzle and reservoir.

Joseph's mind drifted away from the lamps. "Do you think the daggerman will sell many of his weapons?"

Zadok, who had been giving quick answers to questions about

his craft, now hesitated and chewed for awhile. "Yes, all of them. Our land rolls in a constant fever of unrest. Our people, knowing that they were chosen by God, will not rest under the domination of a pagan nation.

Joseph said, "This condition must make it inviting for any revolutionary who can gain a following to call himself the Messiah." He watched the potter turn from the conversation to his shelf of lamps.

"Next I place the piece on this shelf with the other greenware to be dipped and fired."

"Why is the dip necessary?" Joseph asked, trying to forget daggers.

"It must have a smooth surface. This feature is important for looks as well as utility; it holds oil better. Watch me, and in a few minutes I will dip all these waiting pieces. I will put them into a diluted mixture of the same clay; it gives them a less porous and more finished surface." Zadok smiled. "You have watched so carefully that I think I could make a potter of you within a few days."

Joseph tried not to return a frown for his host's smile. Until that moment, he had been fascinated with the craft; but when he himself was offered a chance to become a potter, the dew of glamour quickly evaporated from the objects. He wanted to roam God's Promised Land. He rejected the thought of being chained by duty to a potter's wheel every day.

Joseph had to force himself to pay attention as Zadok showed him the kiln, where the greenware would be fired. To the imaginative young man, the kiln was a cocoon, where the wiggling clay would be transformed into the fixed beauty of pottery. The heat of the oven, like the heat of his mother's dyeing vats, made him thirsty for a drink from the hanging waterskin.

Each evening before their meal, the boy came by and asked, "Are you going tonight?" Each night, Zadok and Sarah replied that it would be impossible.

One night, Zadok said to Jacob, "Perhaps one of us can go tomorrow night, and soon both can return to the fellowship." The boy, happy with the answer, said that he might remain with Zadok for supper if it would not be an imposition. To this suggestion, the potter said, "We would count it a privilege to have you, but we wouldn't want you to miss the love feast." The boy, perhaps encouraged by the aroma of chicken stewing in onion broth, decided he would break bread with them.

Someone at the table asked Joseph what Cyprus was like. The question was like releasing the door of a dove's cage. His answers came soaring. He relished an opportunity to tell about the wonderful land of his birth; he called it a ripened pomegranate in the blazing sun. He regaled them with a description of its climate, its beauty, and its Hebrew people. He omitted any reference to its patron goddess, Aphrodite, which fact a native of Greek ancestry would bring out first. He assured them that the Jews were treated well on the Roman-dominated island.

While they were completing the meal with slices of honey cake, Joseph asked Zadok about the Messiah. Zadok stopped chewing and responded with a simple story. He told about the life and death of Jesus of Nazareth, supplying just enough information to sound completely absurd to the Cypriot Jew.

Their conversation was interrupted by a man—obviously not a stranger—wearing a beautiful cloak with sky-blue stripes woven into it. He asked Zadok for a shipment of lamps. When Zadok left the room to go to his workshop, the stranger said to Sarah, "I want you to sew a dress for my wife."

"I think I can find the time. What does she want?"

"When she first joined the Followers of the Way, she gave away all her finest gowns. Now she doesn't feel comfortable in the rough woolen garments that she has left." He was pacing the floor as he talked.

"I will try to please her, Brother Ananias."

"By the way, I have not seen you in the fellowship recently."

She paused, and Joseph joined the conversation. "I am afraid that these wonderful people have given up all their regular duties in order to nurse me back to health. Now that I have recovered, I would like for them to continue their regular activities."

Zadok returned with two woven baskets stuffed with lamps,

66

"Yes, we will return soon."

After he left, no one felt like continuing the supper conversation. Sarah began to clean off the table, and the boy left for his grandmother's house.

Zadok placed a bowl over the lamp on the table and extinguished its light without blowing oil on to the table. For a long time he and Joseph sat staring at the bowl, almost as if they were looking through it to the smothered light beneath. The only other illumination in the room came from another lamp in a wall niche.

Joseph asked, "Who is this Ananias?"

The potteryman answered. "He does not come from around here. About six years ago, he and his wife moved to Jerusalem from Alexandria. They seem like Romans, they talk like Greeks, they look like Egyptians, and yet they are Jews.

"I notice that he is quite energetic."

The older man observed, "Yes, but that energy would run down, if he were not speeded up by the spurs of his wife. She is a very ambitious woman. Like the women of Rome, she expects her husband to provide her with the luxuries of the world."

"I would like to see her."

"You will. She frequently comes with him to select lamps. It always takes longer when she comes. She is very careful and will accept no flaw, unless I offer the article for half price."

"I see," Joseph said, half critically and half enviously.

Zadok continued, "I wish that Ananias could come under the yoke of steady employment. About five years ago, he bought a beautiful piece of land on a hill just west of the Holy City. He planted an orchard of baby olive trees. He had saved up the money in Egypt, where he supplied cosmetics. When he came here to look at the property, he was clearly told that it would take twenty years before he could realize a profitable harvest; but he said he could wait. Now, he and his wife, Sapphira, are much too impatient for olives. They have no children to leave the valuable investment to, and recently, he has been trying to sell it. Not many Jews have enough to buy it. Perhaps a wealthy foreigner will. In the meantime, he has been buying my lamps, acting as my broker. Before he started, I was producing many more than I could sell here at my little stand. Now he comes for as many as I can produce, working every day but the sabbath. He takes them away by the basketfull."

"What does he do with them?"

"He takes them to Caesarea and to Tiberius. There are many Jewish families in both places who do not want to buy the Augustan lamps with mythological figures and elaborate designs on them. They, like the Jews here, prefer the simple Herodian lamp."

"Is he making a profit?"

"Definitely. In Tiberius, he usually sells the lamps to dealers for cash, although once in awhile he brings back a load of salted fish from the Sea of Galilee in exchange. But in Caesarea, he refuses cash and brings back glass objects—flasks, vials, even large goblets. Here, look at this piece he gave me. It is too beautiful to use and risk breaking. I keep it high on this shelf." Like a priest in a mystic ceremony, he carefully held the glass and reverently handed it to his guest.

Joseph reached out to receive the beautiful honey-colored goblet with two handles near the top. He saw that his hand was trembling. Quickly, he returned the fragile ornament to the old man before he dropped it.

"People here are willing to pay fabulous prices for these. Remember what Job said, talking about a cruder kind of glass than this: 'Even gold and glass cannot equal wisdom.' It is not made anywhere in this sacred land. It must be imported from Tyre, Sidon, or Byblos." The lecturer reminded him of his rabbi, but his movements were more steady. The potter returned the lovely piece of glass to its shrine on the shelf. Then with genuine concern, he said, "Joseph, my son, you are getting better. If you are well enough tomorrow, I would like to take you to the Temple."

The next day was one of dazzling beauty. Because Joseph had been inside the potter's house each morning during his period of convalescence, he had not discovered how fresh was the air that blew over Jerusalem early in the morning. It cooled his unshaven face. This time of day was, he learned, the time that Jesus' followers liked to gather at the Temple, before they themselves went to work and before the place was crowded with many other people.

He hated to leave Sarah to return to the place that had caused him so much pain. The head injury he had received there had taken many days to heal. His disappointment could not be remedied as quickly; he knew that it might become a chronic illness in his thinking, a permanent detriment to his Jewish life. He wondered if he could ever love the Temple and yearn for its courts again.

When they entered the gate, Joseph again saw the beggars except for the one he thought he knew. As they crossed the courtyard of the Gentiles, he paid no attention to the money changers nor to the sellers of sacrificial birds and animals. His eyes went to the balustrade with its warnings, and his mind flew back to his previous visit. He had not inquired about the fate of the Greek slave, for he did not want confirmation of the answer he suspected.

They went to the portico that stretches along the east side toward the Mount of Olives. With its three rows of columns down a long marble corridor, it made an excellent place for the believers to meet. Everything about the place seemed appropriate: ample space and magnificent surroundings.

The service began with familiar Jewish prayers said from memory and readings, from the law and the prophets. Then Peter and James were given an opportunity to tell something about their recollections of Jesus. At the conclusion of the service, which Joseph did not quite understand, they were all invited to attend an upper room service that evening. He understood even less about the reference to the upper room and cared little to find out, for he knew that he would not attend.

As they left the Temple, he looked out on the hills and saw hundreds of tents and flimsy booths. People were celebrating their past. They were reliving the wilderness wanderings, recalling its simple life and recognizing their absolute dependence on God.

When the sun started to set and the sky turned the color of pink oleander, Sarah came to the bed on which he was resting. "Please come with us to the upper room tonight."

"For some people worshiping twice in one day is all right, but not for me. I received enough blessing this morning to last me a long time." He started to make a joke about the meeting, but stopped when he saw how seriously she was taking it.

"I hoped that you, especially, would go with us." She made the invitation sound very personal.

Afraid that he would appear ungrateful to his nurse, he said, "It will be a pleasure to go with you." He gathered up his robe, and he could feel the coins inside it. He did not trust them to be left in the empty house.

He was glad that it was not far to the house of the upper room. They went down the narrow, turning road that takes one to the western edge of the city. There on a ridge were several larger homes, each with high walls outside. When Joseph entered a gate with the others, he found a courtyard with fig trees and grape vines. They went up an outside flight of stairs to the strangest gathering he had ever attended.

All the guests were seated around tables, not reclining in the usual Roman fashion, because there was not enough room, but simply sitting. They were preparing to eat a meal.

The potter explained, "Each night a different group comes here for a meal and the memorial. We have seven workers; each one is in charge a different night with his own helpers."

Suddenly, Joseph felt a thumping in his chest. He thought he saw his own mother standing at the landing of the inside stairs, directing the men with their hot platters of food. He knew that he must be dreaming again, as he had done so often in recent days on the little cot in the potter's house. Yet this apparition seemed different, more tangible and realistic.

With childish innocence, he rushed to the woman and asked, "Who are you?"

A kind voice answered, "I am Mary, the widow of Eleazar."

Joseph, with his heart pounding even faster, motioned with his hands and raised his voice, as if he were speaking to a deaf person. "Do you have a sister in Cyprus with the name of Abigail?"

"Yes, I have not seen her in twenty years. Tell me about her." She grabbed his arm.

Joseph smiled, conscious that his hair had fallen into ringlets of black curls against his forehead, "I am her son."

There was a long embrace and some tears that reflected light from the wall torches. She inquired of her sister's health. Then she introduced Joseph to his cousin, her only son, John Mark. He was much shorter than Joseph and several years younger, perhaps not even twenty, he guessed.

"Then you are little Joseph." She sounded just like his mother, but he heard her words with no embarrassment. He was pleased to be part of a family again.

Joseph apologized for the two weeks' growth of beard, which they said made no difference. The woman suggested he sit down at a table and talk to them while others were eating. During the meal, he told of his going to the Temple. Before he got to the part about his accident, he made some remarks about his disappointment with the Temple.

His cousin nodded approval, and his aunt interrupted, "The Messiah was also displeased. He said that his Father's house was to be a house of prayer for all people."

For a solemn moment, Joseph remembered the poor slave who had been dragged away by the mob. Then his thoughts returned to her recounting of the Messiah's overthrowing the tables of the money changers and releasing the birds for sacrifice, with a great flutter of white wings. Joseph felt sympathy for the actions of this brave Messiah, whom she seemed to respect.

He told about his accident and the hospitality of Zadok the potter. The kind woman could not wait for him to finish but hugged both Zadok and Sarah as they were eating.

As his mother's sister told him about the new religion she had found, Joseph looked at the other tables. It seemed like the happiest meal he had ever attended. People were genuinely interested in one another. No one tried to make a glutton of himself or to drink all the wine. There were no loud, obstreperous voices, as in a Roman banquet. There was no idle flirtation between married women and other men. There was no music in the background, yet all was happiness and enjoyment.

71

He noticed at the main table an empty place, set with a handsome silver chalice and a plate of unleavened bread.

When the meal was concluded, an imposing person he remembered from the Temple, Peter, stood up and broke off a piece of the unleavened bread. He passed the remainder in both directions. Next he held aloft a chalice of silver, said a blessing over it, and took a sip. The chalice passed from one person on to the next. When it came to him, he was hypnotized by the container. He had seen wine served in his home each sabbath eve from a beautiful container. Yet this one was different. Because each person had handled it so reverently, he expected to see a miraculous potion in it; instead, he saw plain, sparkling wine. He dared not put it to his lips. He passed it to John Mark, who better understood its contents.

Peter spoke: "As you know, we do not take a collection when we meet in the Temple. We prefer to receive from our own people in a quiet way that does not attract attention or danger. Several of our men have been thrown out of work because of their new faith. They are suffering, and their families are hungry. As long as we are able, we should help our brothers and sisters in the faith. Those who would gladly give may now do so." A young man, still in his teen years, stepped to the front of the room, and placed on the table in front of the disciple a handsome dagger with a carved ivory handle. He was not the same stranger with the shock of hair who had come to the potter's house, but his dagger had been kept for the same purpose.

He murmured loud enough for those near the front to hear, "I will not be needing this any longer."

Then a striking woman, with hard lines around her lips, sauntered forward and placed on the table a pair of elaborate earrings. She said nothing. After a pause, an elderly man laid two shekels on the table.

"It seems this will complete the giving tonight," said Peter, "unless someone else feels led by the Spirit to make a contribution for these meals and to help pay the expenses of our brethren who cannot support themselves."

Joseph could not remain seated. He reached for his cloak. He stepped over the bench on which he was sitting and felt himself coasting toward the apostle as smoothly as a chariot pulled along by four fine horses.

Everyone stared at his cloak. He felt that he must explain, "I am not giving the cloak; I will be needing it. But there is something inside I will not be needing. I want to present it to the Messiah, to be used for his brothers and sisters."

He was not weeping; he was not hysterical. His mind was clear, and he was happy.

He did not care to lay his offering on the table with the others, for he felt it did not represent as much a sacrifice as the lad's instrument of violence or the woman's bangles. He had known all along he would someday give this money to God, but he had not understood the manner. Now it was clear to him. Joseph knelt before Peter and unwrapped the cloak. The lovely coins began to spill out next to the apostle's bare feet. One hundred and twenty pieces reflected the flickering rays of the lamps. Someone behind him drew in her breath in a gasp. Then a murmur filled the place. The disciples asked, "Are you sure this is what you want to do?"

"Yes, it is God's money."

Many things were happening to Joseph that seemed as if they had happened before in his dreams. Exhilirated, he was pleased with his deed, but he did not care for the attention. The combination of embarrassment and happiness reminded him of his wedding day, when the men of his neighborhood had paraded with him to the home of his bride. On that distant day, he had compensated for his timidity by waving his sword in the air and singing at the top of his voice. People had called him drunk, but he knew that he had not taken even a sip of wine. Just now, he felt the same way, extremely happy, almost inebriated without the assistance of strong drink. He was in full control of his faculties.

He felt the hug of the large fisherman and then a pushing away as the Apostle looked him in the eye. He saw the glint of tears in Peter's eyes but heard no hoarseness in his mighty voice as he said, "The Lord once said to me, 'Thou art Peter, the Rock,' and I was

73

never again the same. In his name, I say to you, 'Thou art Barnabas, son of encouragement.' "

There followed a long moment of intense silence. He pondered his old name, "Joseph," which meant "May God add." His parents had chosen the name for him in the fond hope that they would be blessed with many grandsons. He had grown so accustomed to the sound of "Joseph" that he had not thought of its actual meaning in a long time. Many of his friends had the same name. It was so common in the Jewish community of Salamis that a man had to be designated by his profession or his hometown: Joseph the cobbler, Joseph the coppersmith, Joseph of Paphos, and Joseph of Syria. Now, silent and withdrawn before a room full of people, he contemplated the significance of a new name.

Barnabas listened for the sound of the people in the room, but he could not hear them. Neither could he see them, for his eyes were focused on Peter's. Barnabas felt a throbbing in his head and felt as if he were again going under water. Afraid that he might faint and destroy the reverence of the meeting, bringing dishonor to his newly discovered family, he reached out for Peter's two arms. The apostle responded with a strong grip on both his arms. To the congregation, it looked like a fraternal embrace. But the few moments gave Barnabas the opportunity to find his moorings and steady his brain.

Others wanted to follow the example of their leader and offer the newcomer congratulations. Every person in the room came by to kiss him on the cheek, to grasp both his arms in embrace, and to call him by his new name. The people were warm and sincere. One of the Sons of Thunder, John, introduced himself and then presented the mother of Jesus, a woman who was not old but appeared quite feeble. She had to be carried down the steps in a chair after she had spoken to the Cypriot. He did not remember any of the other names, except, of course, the ones he already knew: Sarah, Zadok, John Mark, and Ananias. Even in his ecstasy, Barnabas noticed one person lingering at the back of the room. She was a woman with a long neck and lifted chin. She was not beautiful, but she had the bearing of an empress. Then he remembered:

74

she had not cared to kiss Barnabas and call him by name, but she had come past him for the handshake. He wondered.

Then he saw a man offer her his arm. It was Ananias, the lamp salesman. They left without saying goodnight to anyone. No one else noticed their departure. All of the others, animated and smiling, were busy talking about the events of the evening.

The night had hardly ended before the next day began for busy Barnabas. Events were piling up, like chariots in a circus wreck. He had given his treasure and identified himself with the Followers of the Way. Then, he learned that the day would be a time of baptismal pilgrimage for himself and others who had joined the believers within the last month. Thus, he slept little during the few hours he was on his bed. He joined the group of candidates heading for the Jordan River, some twenty miles distant.

The believers left from the Dung Gate long before sunrise. Most of the men in the group walked, but Barnabas was not yet strong enough and rode Olivia. John Mark went, leading a donkey loaded with baptismal robes his mother had sewn. They processed past Bethany in the blackness of predawn. Just after the sun came up, gleaming more than a new coin from the emperor's mint, they stopped at the half-way inn. After watering their animals, they continued the descent to the Jordan Valley. Even during the early morning, Barnabas perspired freely, and after they reached the sub-sea level depression, he felt as if he would suffocate.

He followed his new friends to the sacred stream. He found himself in the line of people stretching from the riverbank out to midstream, where a bearded apostle asked each candidate, "What do you believe?"

Each one professed a belief, well instructed by a catechetical leader as to his choice of words. Barnabas had had little time to memorize a statement of belief, but he was unworried. As the line diminished, he found himself in the strong arms of the disciple, being lowered back to the water level, with the cool current combing through his hair and flowing past his bearded chin.

He was pushed down into the cleansing flux. He knew that it was only a moment that he was under the surface of the Jordan

75

River, but the instant was full of thoughts. He felt as if he were once again in the crystal, green waters off Caesarea. Without worry about rising to the surface, he enjoyed the cool relief for his warm head and relaxed in the firm grip that sustained him.

He came up from the rite, feeling no different, yet deeply satisfied. He received a new white robe as he came from the river and let his wet clothes drop in the ooze at the water's edge. He wore the robe to the service held near the bushes of the riverside. The service there was simple and instructive, undistinguished except for the presence of four visitors from the nearby monastic community of Qumran. The informal ceremony ended with the singing of a hymn.

Most of the believers decided to camp at the Jordan's edge or spend the night in Jericho. One convert, a stonemason, said that he had to be back in Jerusalem for his work the next day. John Mark, who also wanted to return, surprised Barnabas with a whispered remark: "I have never spent the night away from home, and I see no need to do so tonight." The three of them, therefore, started on the toilsome climb back up the serpentine road to the Holy City.

Before the sun parted company with them, Barnabas began to yawn. His shoulders drooped. Like a prodigal who had overspent his resources, Barnabas had no energy left to spend on the trip.

After dark the stonemason said that he was not sweating as much, but Barnabas heard him dragging his sandals. Simultaneously, the thrump-thrump of the donkey's hoofs in the powdery dust slowed to an irksome pace. John Mark, the youngest, walked ahead of the others in the dark climb. He had left his animal for one of the older women to ride back.

From one end to the other, Barnabas's body felt conquered. His head ached, and he had become dizzy. His stomach was nauseous, and the trio had to stop two or three times because of it.

In the blackness of the early morning, they came into Jerusalem through the one little gate that was left open. The town was asleep behind closed windows and bolted doors when they parted to go to their separate residences. John Mark tried to get Barnabas to come with him, but Barnabas said he felt at home at the potter's, and he was able to get there without assistance. With energy dissipated, the newly-baptized Christian felt the chill of early morning air. As he opened the familiar door, he wondered how much longer he would call the potter's house his home.

V.

Barnabas—it was a name that had magic rubbed on it. Women repeated the charmed word as they drew water from Jerusalem's wells. Children, hearing it and liking the sound, chanted "Barnabas" as they skipped in circles. Coarse workmen swore with it, finding "by the hands of Barnabas" easier to say than "by the beard of the high priest." Whenever a follower referred to him in connection with another believer, he always put this name first. It was "Barnabas and Zadok" or "Barnabas and John Mark." A speaker-for-God once pointed to his generosity as an example of Christlike selflessness, but Barnabas felt compelled to contradict him, even in a large meeting with most of the apostles present. He wished he could stop the enchanters.

Barnabas had given all he had. He was neither ashamed of the fact, nor proud. However, he felt the deep pleasure of an athlete who has given all his energy in order to master an event. The ensuing tiredness, with its satisfaction, pushed from his mind any worry. "I simply did what I felt was right," he explained, as if he felt a need to justify his action.

People wanted to honor him. Someone—Barnabas suspected Zadok—sent to the Twelve a request to make him an apostle. It seemed strange that Peter would appear suddenly one night at the potter's house and begin explaining, "The requirements for an apostle are that he must have accompanied Jesus in his teaching days as a disciple and must have witnessed a resurrection appearance. The circle is closed."

Even from the next room Barnabas could hear Zadok's answer, "I can understand. Sometimes, my brother, I am not sure that the Twelve did the right thing in electing another to fill Judas' vacancy. Matthias is a sincere follower, but his memory is not clear, and each time he retells a miracle, it has different background details. Perhaps it is better if the circle is closed."

Barnabas was relieved that the apostolic idea was stillborn. He had doubts about the honor he had purchased. After the leader's departure, he confided to Zadok, "These compliments worry me."

The potter advised, "Accept them, and forget them. When someone compliments my lamps I don't take credit; I simply say that the craft is a trade I inherited, a family legacy. If I grew proud over a complimented lamp, I would be stealing the praise from one of my ancestors who invented this design. And, besides, if I grew proud over one lamp, I would be sure to mar the next one."

"I feel exactly that way about the honor. Much of the money I inherited from my father. I simply did what needed to be done with it. I am afraid that the attention will detract from the stature of the apostles."

"Do not worry about them. Their place is secure." The potter cleared his throat as he made the statement, and he did not sound as positive as his words seemed to indicate.

The believer from Cyprus felt over-rewarded. Appraising himself unworthy of the honors, he tried harder to live up to the kind statements the widows made about him. He visited in homes all over the Holy City, going from Ophel to Mount Moriah, from the Sheep Gate to the Dung Gate. He offered encouragement to the bereaved, who treasured a visit and told about it in the evenings to follow. His zeal could not catch up with the compliments; it simply produced more praise.

Visitors stopped by the potter's to visit with Barnabas. They wanted him to feel welcomed to their town and their Christian fellowship. They asked his advice on the weather and commented on Zadok's lamps. It seemed that mainly they stopped in to hear his encouraging, enthusiastic greetings: not just a single *shalom,* but the triple repetition of "Peace, peace, peace be unto you," each note rising on the musical scale.

Barnabas, once again clean shaven, felt like working. He avoided the crafting of lamps for some shadow of a reason in the front of his mind, but he volunteered to levigate the clay. Grinding, sifting, kneading, he prepared the raw material with a baker's care. Meticulously he added water. Then he mixed and pressed the wet

79

mass, carefully working out all air bubbles that would leave holes in the finished product.

He often said, "I prefer manual tasks to skilled work."

Zadok, deeply appreciative, replied, "I am not able to do all of this by myself. I don't know what I would do without you. My time is limited, and I can't wait forever for the boy to become my apprentice."

Barnabas, insisting that he was strong enough, began to learn the routine of firing the kiln. He was surprised to find that it was not a daily process, but a weekly ritual. First, the dried pieces of pottery had to be stacked up in the rear of the kiln, near the chimney. Then the slow fire was started between the pottery and the door of the kiln. This was the most tedious process of the whole routine. For Barnabas discovered on his first attempt, when he made the fire too rapidly, that it broke a whole kiln full of lamps.

On a second try with a slow buildup period, he kept a metal cover over the chimney, just as Zadok had instructed, although he wondered why. After twelve hours, however, Zadok told him to remove the cover, and pile in soft wood that would burn quickly. "This is the period of blasting," he tersely explained. The softwood fire sucked in a draft and sent a tumbling fountain of smoke high into the Jerusalem sky. Neighbors for quite a distance nodded with approval, when they saw the evidence of the potter's successful industry.

Next came the period for patience. Barnabas had to let the fire burn slowly for the next three days and finally smolder out. This final phase was the most difficult, to wait to see if he had spoiled the lamps with too hot a fire or too fast an ignition.

Sarah, Zadok, and Barnabas crowded about the mouth of the kiln to see the opening. After the bricks were removed from the entrance, they found the entire batch in perfect shape, with color, hardness, and durability to match.

It was during one of these waiting periods that Barnabas first met the woman he had asked about. He had replaced the lid on the chimney and the fire was burning quietly, in contrast to the frenzied blasting, which was now long since completed. Zadok came back to the courtyard to check on the kiln's temperature frequently, inquiring each time about Barnabas' holding out. When he appeared satisfied, he returned to his wheel to whirl out a new creation that was an identical twin to the last one he had created.

On one occasion, he came hurrying back to the kiln. "Barnabas, Barnabas." His long nose was highlighted by the glare of the unfiltered light of the courtyard.

The Cypriot was about to object to this solicitude, when he saw that the potter approached for a different purpose. He had with him Sapphira. She was dressed like a peasant, but she walked regally. She was carrying a handsome red pottery, flat-based dish that was fully two handspans across.

Zadok was excited. "Do you recognize this? It is *terra sigilata,* stamped earth." When he perceived that his helper did not understand, he continued, "It is one of the most beautiful kinds of ceramic in the world. Those potters north of Rome are real artists. I wish that I could see one at work." He pointed to the base. "See the stamp of the potter underneath."

Barnabas nodded a greeting to this sister in the faith and reached for the lovely piece of imported pottery which she offered. He turned the dish upside down and examined a tiny impression that looked like a footprint, about the size of his thumbnail and saw scratched under it a Roman name. "I don't blame the potter for signing this work. It's a masterpiece." He admired the red glaze that covered the surface and took note of the geometric design stamped on the upper side.

"But Brother Zadok, I think your pottery is just as beautiful in a different way," said the woman.

"This is artistry. My lamps cannot be compared with this masterpiece."

"Oh, yes," said Barnabas, "and I think you should stamp some particular mark on the base of your lamps."

The ceramist answered, "It would be unfair to my father who taught me the trade and took no credit for his work. It would also be unfair to the men on the Street of the Potters who turn out identical lamps." The familiar words reminded Barnabas of his own decision to receive no honor or credit for his gift to the church. He hoped that he could remain as modest as the older man.

Barnabas did not immediately give back the platter-dish. Wanting to fondle it longer, he felt a strange affinity for the object. It had come from another country to its destination in the Promised Land. It had resisted being broken on the long voyage. It had been stamped by its maker with a mark as unremovable as that of circumcision. It could bring happiness and satisfaction to new friends in its new home, maybe even encouragement.

He heard Sapphira ask Zadok to copy it for her that she might have several serving pieces. The potter did not seem happy with the request, and the woman sensed his hesitancy. She said, "Please keep the piece for awhile. If you don't care to copy it, I will respect your decision. In the meantime, enjoy it." Barnabas admired her courtesy. He realized that she was a woman with a strong will, but she refused to exert any pressure on this workman. There was something straightforward and frank about her. She had said exactly what she wanted, without resorting to hints or tricks. When she did not get her wish, she indicated that she would wait. As she prepared to leave, she casually said, "It has been quite a while since all our leaders were together for a service. Peter is always off on a mission; so is Philip. And Stephen seems to be in a frenzy of teaching. If he can get even one listener, he will miss a love feast. I would like to see them all together again, like in the former days."

Zadok replied, "I happen to know that the Seven will be present for our next big meeting. When Peter was here the other night, he told me that Stephen will present a plan for contacting new seekers."

Sapphira said, "That sounds like Stephen to want all that attention." When she saw the deep furrows her remark had plowed into Zadok's forehead, she said nothing else about Stephen. "When can we expect the biggest attendance of our believers?"

Zadok said, "I can't be sure, because the meeting on the first day of the week has become very popular. People like the significance of the early morning celebration of the resurrection. Someday it might become our most popular meeting. But I believe at

82

the present time the sabbath eve service is the best attended."

After she left, the enclosure seemed colorless. The cooking kiln looked as repulsive as a giant hog, squatting on the ground. Messy piles of broken pottery, which he had never before noticed, were scattered about the inner yard. The woman had brought an excitement to the place. Sapphira's first visit was the last time Barnabas saw her happy and confident. The circumstances of their next confrontation were so different that the occasion became one of the most bothersome nightmares in the new convert's life.

Since the sabbath started with Friday's sunset, workers in Jerusalem began stopping at midday. Potters and fullers let their fires die down. Stonemasons began the tedious job of scrubbing their hands and washing their hair before putting on clean garments for the Holy Day. Bakers, who had put out their week's largest supply on that morning, remained open until late afternoon, trying to sell their last products before the appearance of three stars would conclude their week.

Women who had begun their preparation early on that morning, managed to have everything cooked in advance, so that no violation of the sparkless day would take place under their roofs. There would be no working by a woman on the sabbath, unless God should send her into the labor of childbirth on that day, a labor which even the most conservative rabbi could not prevent. There would be no whittling, carving, or wrapping on that day, unless it were a week after a male child had been born, and on that day circumcision was required. Otherwise, there were to be no violations of the day of sacred rest and praise.

The believers enjoyed the sabbath. It gave ample opportunity for them to gather for a meal together in the evening and to continue with a service of praise and instruction, free from worry about the next day's commitments. They gathered early at the upper room. Barnabas was glad that he could meet there, because it was a privilege extended to only a few of the new members.

Mostly the old members who felt guided back to that spot, rather than to work with new congregations, worshiped there. On this night in the city of Jerusalem, there were six similar gatherings.

Zadok, in his beautiful sabbath robe, looked years younger than when he hunched over his potter's wheel. Barnabas was wearing a new garment which Sarah had woven for him and made into a robe. The men stopped in the street outside the house of Mary to talk, and Sarah went in to help the deacons with the tables and later to start singing some of the sweet songs of Israel. Barnabas watched for Sapphira to arrive.

The apostle Peter presided at the meeting and announced that James, the son of Zebedee, was conducting a service in the home of Nicodemus. After the converted fisherman gave some of his memories about the teachings of Jesus, he invited anyone who felt led to speak.

Stephen spoke briefly, but in those moments his eyes glowed with a warm brilliance and his tongue seemed touched by some burning coal from an altar of sacrifice. He spoke his brief request for people to win their neighbors and then sat down. Barnabas looked to see Sapphira's reaction, but he could not find her. It was at that moment that he noticed Ananias, looking strangely alone, pushing his way through the crowd to the front, where the apostle was presiding. Barnabas immediately recognized the lamp sales- man, although he had not seen him recently.

He watched Ananias bow with deep reverence. He heard whis- perers in the room grow quiet as the man spoke. "I have sold my olive orchard. I want to give my money to the church." With a sweeping gesture, he deposited an impressive number of coins at the leader's feet.

People in the congregation smiled with approval. Some of the elders murmured their appreciation of the generous act. Peter was silent. Barnabas could not guess what words of commendation Peter would choose for Ananias. He wondered if the apostle would bestow on him a new name, as in that ecstatic moment when he changed "Joseph" to "Barnabas."

The room became saturated with silence. Barnabas wondered

why the apostle was waiting such a long time; usually he spoke out impetuously. The Cypriot saw Ananias straighten up from his humbled position and look with doubt-filled eyes into the apostle's face. Peter's eyes glared back into his. Those terrible eyes seemed to grow larger, framed by a wrinkled brow and a scowling face. Everyone present saw Ananias begin to shiver, as if he were out on a cold mountainside at dawn.

Peter drew in his breath. He yelled the tragic name aloud, "Ananias." It seemed that he was speaking to someone falling into an abyss.

A questioning moan escaped through the thin slit in Ananias' lips.

Peter continued, "Why has Satan filled your heart to lie to the Holy Spirit and to keep back part of the proceeds of the sale? While it remained unsold, did it not remain your own possession? And after it was sold, was it not at your disposal? How is it that you have contrived this deed in your heart?"

While the words of clear truth were ringing out in that sacred assembly, the poor wretch began to chant over and over, "No, no, no, no." He grabbed the ankles of the apostle, as if to keep from falling into a deep pit.

Peter's voice then dropped to a loud whisper. "You have not lied to men but to God." The shivering man stopped shaking. His moaning grew silent. His greedy hands unclasped the ankles of the holy apostle. He collapsed in a heap, like a bag of entrails from a butcher's slaughterhouse. Awaiting a gesture from their leader, several strong young men came forward and took his body out for burial.

The meeting turned into an ordeal for the believers. They felt terror and awe. Something beyond their explanation and comprehension was taking place. Several agitated and tearful worshipers asked for chances to apologize to the congregation for past actions.

John Mark went to Peter and whispered something in his ear. Then the leader asked the members to listen to this young man and to pray for him. Barnabas noticed that his cousin, John Mark, had great difficulty in expressing himself. He got across the idea

85

that he had not been doing enough for the cause of the Messiah, and he wanted to do more, if he could find the guidance to do it. In reassuring words, Peter said to him, "Our Shepherd will guide us."

Barnabas was too stunned to speak. His mind could not find its way out of the spiritual maze of events. He could not concentrate on the words of the service which seemed brief, but he knew it must have lasted some two or three hours. When it was concluded, no one left. Everyone stood around talking, each telling how the death affected him. Then they suddenly stopped.

The wife of Ananias appeared in the doorway that came up from the courtyard, the same opening through which the man's body had been carried. At the first moment in the doorway, she wore a smile. Then when no one returned her smile, she looked confused. Barnabas began to push his way to her. Someone must tell her of the awful events. Someone must warn her not to make a fool of herself with a similar lie. He did not like the assignment, but he knew it must be done. He wanted to take her to the quiet courtyard below and explain the terrible circumstances. Then, perhaps, he could encourage her to enrol as one of the widows of the church, certainly the youngest, but she could set an example by her service and receive a continual upkeep from the concerned congregation. She could help to nurse the sick and to prepare food for the love feasts.

"I must talk to you."

"Later," said Sapphira.

"This matter cannot wait. Come with me to the courtyard below."

"Why has no one grabbed me by the arm to congratulate me?" She was wearing the magnificent new fabric Ananias had given to Sarah to make for her. She looked like a woman of Rome, ready to make a public appearance, dressed to impress the plebians. Gently but firmly she pushed Barnabas aside and marched toward the arena of truth.

Peter motioned for her to come to him so that he could ask her something. Again the upper room was enveloped by the stillness of the grave. The worshipers looked at her as if they had seen someone returned from the silence of the tomb.

Like a judge, the sacred leader asked very clearly a straightforward question, "Tell me whether you sold the property for this amount at my feet?" No one had touched the evil coins, and they remained in the same place where they had been deposited by the schemer.

She paused, and Barnabas hoped that she would glance his way long enough for him to motion for her to tell the truth. He feared however, that she would find no reason in her heart to confess and that she would likely perpetuate the lie. Although he knew the words were forthcoming, he experienced a tearing and ripping inside his soul as he heard her say, "Yes, for that amount."

Not so much in anger but with a broken heart, Peter began, "How is it possible?" He stopped for a moment and began anew with even more agitation and fury. "How is it that you have agreed together to tempt the spirit of the Lord?"

The woman started shaking her head in a vigorous denial. Peter's words were like an uncontrollable tumble of rocks off a mountainside. "Listen! The feet of those who buried your husband are at the door, and they will carry you out, also."

In the sepulchral silence, everyone could hear the young men removing their sandals on the wooden platform outside the door. It was an ordinary sound. But, under the circumstances, it was transformed into a ghostly ritual. Even more eerie was the noise that came from Sapphira. Like the last wind leaving a bellows when its usefulness is over, the breath was exhaled from her body, and she dropped to the floor. In those terrifying moments, her heart stopped, and the prediction came true.

Someone whispered a word, a strangely recognizable word, "anathema." It had never before been used in a meeting of the Followers of the Way. On this occasion, it seemed appropriate. To the mind of Barnabas, it hinted of the primitive rite in which the carcass of an animal is hung in a sacred tree. While suspended, it is dedicated for destruction and later cut down and burned. These deceivers had been accursed and cut off in a similar way.

The same ones who had carried away the body of Ananias now picked up the limp corpse that had recently been Sapphira. The spectators remained motionless and silent. Then Barnabas heard his aunt begin a hymn of praise. He could not endure listening to music after two people had died tragically.

Barnabas left the room by the other door, and Zadok followed him. At the bottom of the stair, where the scent of baking bread still lingered, he turned fiercely to the potter. "This thing is terrible. It is just as bad as gladiatorial combat which they all denounce." Zadok did not answer but placed a paternal hand on Barnabas' shoulder. He had the feeling that the potter did not understand, and his horror turned to a rage. "If this is the way of Jesus then I am through with it. If this is the approach of Peter, the church's greatest leader, then I . . ." Even in his fury, Barnabas did not want to offend Zadok, his benefactor, but he knew that he had to express these feelings that were too powerful to cage. ". . . I offer him no respect."

Zadok led him over to a bench under a fig tree. When they both were seated, he said, "Peter did not kill these unfortunate people. He is no murderer. Neither is he a gladiator who kills for money or kills to keep from being killed. Ananias and Sapphira committed spiritual suicide."

Barnabas said, "Yes, they made a mistake, but they paid a terrible price for it. They received a major punishment for a trivial matter of money."

"It was not for money, but for their deceit. Tonight Peter minted a phrase that I predict will be used whenever this event is retold; he said, 'They lied to the Holy Spirit.' "

The singing stopped. A female voice started reciting praises in a frenzied chant. Other voices joined in the shouting. Barnabas smiled, "Interesting. They are draining off their excitement in shouting, and I am getting rid of mine by talking to you of my horror and disgust."

A person from a neighboring courtyard yelled, "Listen to the donkey-worshipers braying."

Zadok said, "I must return to the upper room before this enthusiasm gets out of hand."

Barnabas, who had just begun to express his feelings, not caring to remain in the courtyard alone and refusing to return to the scene of the tragedy, started walking. He meandered down the alley-like streets of the Holy City. Over cobblestones and up steps in the street, he ambled. He heard a group of late celebrants singing some ancient tunes, and he turned away toward silence. When he returned to the potter's house and saw the outline of the Temple, brooding over the resting city, he suddenly realized that he had been walking on the sabbath and had surpassed the rule of the thousand paces. Such a matter was a midget compared with the giant that was troubling his mind.

In bed with his eyes squeezed shut, Barnabas kept seeing the events of the evening. They arranged themselves into a patter of flowing lines and melting colors. The tortured design was dominated by three personalities: Sapphira, Peter, and Ananias. He prayed for some vision of the cross to intervene and obscure the terrible scene. He kept seeing the pathetic couple with their cherished money. He wished for the risen Savior to appear and cast out the evil spirits in his memory. Nothing happened.

All night long, he flopped from one side to the other, like a fish on a pier. Just when the fish seems the quietest, completely exhausted, it flips into the air and onto its other side.

In the midst of his grief and doubt, another thought grabbed Barnabas with such force that he sat up in bed and spoke aloud to the black emptiness of the room. "It is *my* fault. I should never have given my money." Immediately after he had spewed out the nauseous idea, he felt better. Yet doubts of its truth began to worry him. He reasoned within himself, silently now, that if he had not given the money when he did, many of the widows might have starved. Besides, others had been helped: orphans, immigrants, and men who had felt discrimination because of their new faith. They needed to eat.

To complicate his dialogue and further confuse his thinking, Barnabas thought of other reasons why he should not have presented the gift. It made these same people dependent and less

89

self-reliant. It had been a temptation to his own pride and desire for acceptance. And he returned to the overpowering thought—it had set a trap in which two ordinary people had been caught and frightened to death.

During the sleepless night he got up and stumbled toward the household's wineskin; he knew approximately where it was hanging, near the far corner of his room. He drank from it like a hungry kid nursing a mother goat. The wine felt warm inside but brought no miracle of new visions.

Sometime after he heard a cock crow, he began planning his schedule for the day. He knew if he remained in Jerusalem, he would only hurt Zadok by arguing with him or by denouncing Peter. It would be better if he left. Too many days had slipped by since he left the old rabbi in pagan Caesarea. He must delay no longer. If he did not return the borrowed ass, he could be accused of stealing her. This particular day would be the ideal time to make his trip to Caesarea.

The journey, he told himself, practicing what he would write in a note to Zadok, would take his mind off Ananias and Sapphira. He went to the courtyard, picked up a broken piece of pottery and wrote his note on the sherd. He left it on his bed. Then he loosened Olivia from her stake and left Jerusalem in the faint glimmer of predawn.

During the quietness of the early morning trip, his mind unrolled the scrolls of his memory, and Barnabas recalled certain Scriptures that emphasized God's cruelty. He thought of the bears that ate children who laughed at the bald-headed Elisha. He thought of the destruction of Achan's entire family. Then his mind dwelt on the invasion of Joshua's slaughtering forces. What kind of God could this be, he wondered.

When he came to Bethel, he found no activity. He had wanted to buy food at the town market. Then he recalled—it was the sabbath. The traveler had always respected the sanctions of the holy day, but now they seemed unreal. He wondered what sort of changes were taking place in his life and how far they would sweep him. He let the donkey nibble on grass by the watering place until children came and threw stones at the sabbath-breakers.

The trip was lonely. He wished for another Roman like Julius. He would even settle for a shepherd and would consent to slowing down his pace for the ambling sheep and would further tolerate the man's flute playing or wool spinning as he walked. But there was no companion available, so he made the trip to Caesarea more quickly than when he had come with Julius of the Augustan Cohort. This time, he rode Olivia during parts of the trip. He slowed his pace only when he came in sight of the great, gaudy, heathen city.

The streets of Caesarea were paved with fine stone, striated to keep the Roman horses from slipping. He passed the hippodrome. Some event must have taken place earlier in the day, for there were still several toga-clad men indolently engaged in discussion. He concluded that these men of wealth had no other important matters to attend to, and he did not mind interrupting them.

Barnabas said to the group, "Please, can you give me directions to the House of the Centaurs?"

The men looked at each other puzzled. Finally, one said, "There is to my knowledge no such house in Caesarea."

A man much shorter than the others said, "Could you mean the House of the Laughing Satyr?"

"Yes, that's the one." Something in Barnabas' memory refused to hang on to mythological references.

"If you were an eagle, you could see it from here," the runt said.

"If I were an eagle, I would not need to ask directions."

The man who first spoke took from his shorter friend the pleasure of giving directions to the traveler. "Travel this street two lengths of a stadium. There you will see a small temple at the top of many steps. It has Ionic columns. That is the Temple of Artemis. Next to it, on the far side, is the House of the Laughing Satyr."

The simple directions were easy to follow. Barnabas noticed the tall flight of steps up to the temple, but he refused to turn his head to look at the repulsive building. He tethered the donkey to an iron ring in the wall beyond the temple and knocked on the door. The polished door was twice as large as Zadok's door and embellished with molding. He looked around the doorframe for a mezuzah, the twenty-two lines of Scripture enclosed in a case which every orthodox Jew puts on his doorpost. The common symbol of Jewry was missing.

The door swung halfway open and an elderly slave with a head of distinguished gray hair asked his business.

"I want to see the father of your mistress."

"Please step inside, and I will call the lady."

Barnabas looked down at the floor of the entranceway and saw in the pleasant mosaic design the Latin word for welcome. He looked past the entrance corridor toward the atrium and thought how different it was from Zadok's courtyard. Here was a place designed for beauty, not employment. He noticed a statue in the middle with close clipped shrubs forming a circle around it.

Then he noticed Cornelia coming from the far side of the court. She looked cool in her light, flowing gown. Her form was framed by the rectangular shadows of the hallway. She did not recognize her visitor until she came into the darkened entranceway.

"Joseph of Salamis." She held out both hands and clasped his. "What has kept you this long?"

"I wanted to come sooner, but I was in an accident."

She loosened one of his hands but tightly held the other to pull him along. "Come, sit in the atrium, and tell me about it." Her friendliness was a contrast to the haughtiness he noticed when he arrived in Caesarea.

Barnabas felt his face getting hot. She was wearing less makeup and no jewels at her neck or ears. Rings on both hands were her only ornaments. He gave a summary of his trip to the Temple and told of running into the beam while chasing Olivia.

"You should have let her go. She is not worth that much."

"She's been very valuable to me. She was almost like a companion on my trip. Later she took me to the river Jordan for baptizing, and . . ."

92

"Surely, you are joking."

"No, I have put my faith in Jesus of Nazareth as the Messiah."

The woman stood. He was expecting her to rave and condemn. However, she appeared bored and said languidly, "Yes, I have heard those stories from the fanatics of Galilee, while his doings were still novel. But they executed him, and that was the end."

"It was not the end but the beginning."

She adjusted a ring that had slipped around on her finger. "Let us talk of more important things. It is almost time for the evening meal. Would you prefer fish or fowl?

"Before I think of food, I want to see the rabbi."

"Very well," she sighed. "Follow me to his room." She led him to one of the rooms opening off the back side of the atrium. The impressively hinged door indicated that it was one of the best accomodations in the home. Barnabas was thankful the teacher had not been cast aside in some animal hovel in the rear. His heart beat faster as she opened the door and invited him to step into the lighted room.

"Here is Father." Lying on a bed was a pale form as withered as a raisin.

Stunned, Barnabas asked, "What has happened to him?"

"He was very weak and feeble, when he arrived. He grew worse. One evening at the table he dropped his food and collapsed in his plate. He has not spoken since and he has not moved his right arm or right leg."

"Can you get him to eat anything?"

Cornelia's face was very solemn as she slowly shook her head.

There was the body of the rabbi, barely alive. This man who had loved to talk, to teach, to exhort, to entertain, now lay wordless, his lips still. He was lying on a freshly made cot, watched over by a slave. But his cheeks were sunken, and his eyes looked like dark caves. His mouth was pulled to one side. He breathed in a kind of wheezing snore. In between the shallow breaths, there were terrifying pauses.

Cornelia called to him several times. Finally, he opened his weary eyelids. The woman placed her lips close to his ear and said,

"Father, Joseph is here. If you can hear me, squeeze his hand."

A moan passed the parched lips of the elder, and the slave rose to put goat butter on them. Bony fingers squeezed Barnabas' hand. There was another sound, halfway between a sob and a cough, then silence. The tired old hand released its grip. His eyes seemed to fix themselves on the ceiling, and they did not respond to anything Barnabas tried to say. His own voice sounded distant and strange.

The rabbi had not departed yet. However, he looked even more like a corpse than had pitiful Ananias, when he was twisted at the feet of Peter. Certainly, the light of the old man's life was giving off its final, faint flickers. His heart was barely pumping, and his chest was still pulling in a small amount of air; but the man was practically dead.

Barnabas' lower lip developed an uncontrollable quiver. His mind dwelt on the despairing thought that he was losing another companion. His father, his own wife, Ananias, and Sapphira had all been removed from his circle of affection by death—now his beloved teacher and fellow traveler. He pictured death as an abominable idol that must be fed on human sacrifice.

Again Barnabas began to reproach himself. There was something inside him that seemed to crave blame. If I had not left him in Caesarea, he thought, this might not have happened. He moved toward the hinged door. "I want to be alone for awhile," he said hoarsely to the rabbi's daughter. She remained in the room, closing the door behind him as Barnabas staggered out into the courtyard. He sat down in the dusk-filled opening and looked at his rough feet, observing the ridges worn by sandal thongs and thinking of the many places he had walked.

The court seemed empty. True, it held no other person. However, there was a statue in the center of the landscaped circle. It was a satyr. The sculpture looked more alive than any he had ever seen before. He admitted that he was no connoisseur, for he had never looked too closely but had averted his eyes in true Hebrew fashion.

This laughing satyr looked like a playing boy, not the lusting, animalistic creature which the name implied—a boy like Rufus or

94

Jacob—romping with his dog. The stone lad was running around the stump of a tree and the dog was just landing on his front feet from a jump. Both were stopped at the instant of almost completed motion—the dog's hind feet still lifted in the air and the boy's full mane of hair flowing from his head like the wake that follows a ship.

Slowly, shadows completely enfolded the sculpture and permitted the visitor's thoughts to return to the rabbi. The teacher might have confided in him, if he had been properly encouraged on the trip, and found cathartic relief for his soul. Now the opportunity was gone. Neither could the rabbi learn of Barnabas' discovery of the Messiah's followers.

Cornelia opened the door, carrying a bronze lamp. She leaned against a column and stared at Barnabas. "Do not brood too much. He has lived a long life, doing what he wanted to. He has helped many people." Words of consolation sounded natural in her throat, but Barnabas knew it was he who should be offering these words of comfort to the rabbi's daughter.

"If I had known that I could hear his voice only one more time, I would have gotten up from my sick bed and traveled day and night to come here."

"You gave me no address to send you news. But don't worry. No one knows the future. And this is a blessing." Again, she was consoling the Son of Encouragement. Barnabas wondered if the man's presence in her household had reclaimed her as a daughter of the covenant. "Come," she said gaily, "let us eat."

He followed her into a banquet room, where she placed the bronze lamp on an ornate stand of the same metal. There were matching braziers of coals at each end of the room, dispelling the damp chill of the seacoast evening. He saw a table set with imported plates and serving pieces, similar to the one Sapphira had brought to the potter to copy. In the center was a large platter of olives, cucumbers, and an item he had never before tried, hard-boiled eggs stuffed with sea urchins.

Couches surrounded three sides of the square table, and the remaining side was left open for slaves to serve. Cornelia reclined on the outside lounge, next to the servant's space, the regular place of the hostess. A slave pointed Barnabas to the middle couch, traditionally used for the guest of honor. Each lounge could hold three guests, and he surmised that she frequently planned parties for nine people. This time there were only two. Although they were propped up on separate couches with their feet toward different walls of the room, their heads were close together at the table. They could reach each other or anything on the table.

Sprawled on a glossy fabric, Barnabas felt uncomfortable. He was about to refuse the luxurious meal, when he considered that any remark might offend his hostess. He glanced at her hips and said nothing. He thought he heard her say, "I have wine from Cyprus." A slave filled their glass goblets. The wine from his island tasted sweet, without the bitter aftertaste of Jerusalem wine. It made him feel warm inside. She told of her refusal to accompany her widowed father to Cyprus many years ago, choosing to remain instead with relatives in Caesarea.

Barnabas, sensing that she was waiting for him to speak, did not care to comment on the rabbi's lonely work in Salamis or his present dying condition. He tried to think of something that did not sound depressing. He knew that he could not make her understand his own departure from the Jerusalem church, for he did not understand it himself. The room was silent, except when the slaves moved about serving and their tunics rustled. Finally, he said, "I was impressed with the statue in your courtyard."

"Since I never had children of my own, he is my child. I would part with any other thing in this house before giving up that sculpture. A visitor from Athens told me that the original of the work is in Greece, and this is a copy. I chose not to believe him. I prefer to think this is the only one in the world. I love its happiness."

Barnabas, impressed by the woman's kindness to him and her devotion to her father, wanted to bridge the gap between them. "I wonder if our ancestors did not lose a lot of beauty in life by condemning sculpture." He knew that she was pleased with the remark, but he feared such an un-Jewish statement might cause

96

the walls to crumble in on them.

He listened to her talk of Caesarean social life during their meal of broiled quail, fish topped with toasted nuts, boiled locust, lentils, cheeses, and fried honeycakes. He noticed that the top of her gown had slipped lower, and he could see more of her body. He tried not to breathe faster. He told himself that he was in an ordinary situation; he tried to think of it as just a meal with a worried friend.

When she started talking about people's ages, he guessed that Cornelia was at least five to ten years older then he, and he hoped he appeared older than his twenty-odd years. "I don't like to talk about my age," she confided, "because it frequently gives me a terrible headache."

The white-haired servant, who had met the door, came in to check on the completion of the meal. When everything seemed to his liking, he dismissed the slaves who served the meal and left with them.

Barnabas looked away from the woman with her fascinating neckline and tried to think rationally. He felt a warm breeze on his face. It was the woman's wine saturated breath. She had pulled herself closer to feed him grapes from a luscious cluster. A peculiar delight carried the breath from his neck throughout his body.

In his anxiety, he ate one grape after another. Then he heard her ask, "Have you ever been married?"

"Yes, my wife died."

"Did you like married life?"

"Yes, I enjoyed it."

"There's nothing wrong with it, although the Essenes raise questions about it." She drew closer, almost on his couch, and spoke in a very serious tone. Barnabas could smell a light fragrance that seemed to originate from her gracefully curved neck. "My husband Yurel was much older than I."

"How did the age difference work out?"

"Not too happily, I am afraid."

"Why did you marry him?"

"He was lonely, and he needed companionship. He had spent his energy in recruiting and training gladiators."

97

"That is a wealthy and influential work," Barnabas said.

"Yes, he grew rich in leasing them for great public shows. Here in Caesarea, people like such affairs. Wealthy people were glad to pay for them in order to win favor with the commoners. But poor Yurel, he worried over his work. When one of his boys would get killed, even if he was just a slave or a prisoner of the wars, he would grieve his heart out. Many nights I have heard him crying quietly in his pillow. All this was such a strain on him; it is no wonder that the Lord afflicted him."

Barnabas, glad to leave behind a discussion of her marriage, dwelt on her final remark. "Do you really think God sends punishment? How about the teaching in the book of Job?"

Cornelia said, "I know little of the Scriptures, but I know I performed a wife's duty. His condition, after he was stricken, was just as bad as my father's is now. I did everything that was necessary for the man, while he lay in that same room, with no use of his left arm and leg. And his pathetic attempt at speech sounded like his mouth was chewing a large hunk of raw beef. I nursed him just like a baby." She paused and let her mood become less sober. "And I remained true to him the entire time." She raised her eyebrows, as if to ask if he believed her.

Barnabas was completely ignorant of what to reply. Eventually, he broke the silence. "Did you call a physician for your husband?"

"Indeed, yes. We have a very fine surgeon here, with many wonderful instruments. But he told me there was nothing he could do." Abruptly, she asked, "Do you have a woman back home?"

"Yes."

He thought he heard her sigh with disappointment.

"My mother."

"I mean, do you have a *special* girl, your betrothed?"

For the first time since he left the potter's shop, he thought of Sarah. She was a *special* friend. She had nursed him back to health. He was indebted to her. "There is a girl I have been living with."

"Ho," she exclaimed, in a sustained throaty note. "You are not so holy after all, living with a wench."

"No, please do not mistake my meaning. I have been living in

98

the same house with an old man and his granddaughter. She is much younger and has been like a little sister to me." As he said these words, they did not sound true. Barnabas knew that Sarah was more to him than a little sister. He recalled those early days of consciousness, when he adored her. She had been a ministering angel to him. Then, as he had been able to get away from the little house, he had thought less and less of her. She had done nothing to disappoint him, but maybe this disinterest had resulted from her quietness. He couldn't tell this sophisticated citizen of Caesarea about his tangle of feelings toward Sarah nor his disappointment with the church, which he had joined and deserted.

Cornelia, warmed by the meal and wine, pushed up the flimsy sleeves of her gown. Her arms were naked and appealing. She said, "It would not be difficult for a woman to fall in love with you."

He responded so instantly that he surprised himself. "And it wouldn't be difficult for a man to love you."

"Do you enjoy being with me?" She smiled.

"Yes. You're lovely, and you've been kind to me. I'm grateful for this delicious meal." He glanced away from her gaze. "I never thought I'd like being with you."

Her lips, again serious and almost closed, were full and crimson. She was breathing through them. He wondered how he could have disliked her at their first meeting on the wharf. She reached her soft hand over to his shoulder and let it rest there.

Barnabas began to feel a thumping in his chest, just as he had when he looked from the Temple wall over the Kidron valley. He sensed danger. The skin on his chest began to tighten. He had not admitted any feeling of desire for a long time, but he felt the return of the intense hunger he had known as a boy of sixteen or seventeen. He put his hand on hers in a quick, rough gesture. She seemed delighted.

She rolled over and looked toward the ceiling. "This is the moment I've yearned for."

Barnabas had an intense desire to pull her to his couch. He wanted to sniff her smooth neck and kiss it. He wondered at what moment he would lose control and follow his passions. In alarm, however, he began to draw back from this enticing nymph. "We must not."

"Yes, my dear boy. You're attracted to me, and I desperately need you. We crave each other."

He rolled over on his stomach, propped up on his elbows and put his chin in his hands. "It is not lawful."

The simple movement of his body away from hers must have seemed like a rejection, for she began to retaliate. "I thought you were such a man. Where is that virility I guessed at under your robe?"

Barnabas felt like an arrow of lightning had struck him. At first, he could not move or think. Then disgust began to bubble from inside him. He closed his mind to her coarse words and said, "I'll go now. I will pay you for the donkey."

"No. I would not touch your money. There is something wrong with you. Something strange. Take that stubborn donkey with you. If it is left here, I will have it destroyed."

"I wanted to help you with your father."

"Leave," she said.

"I wanted to talk to you of religion."

"Leave," she commanded in a scream so loud that slaves opened the doors to check on her safety.

Barnabas wished that he could see his rabbi one more time, but he knew that Cornelia would not permit it. He wished he had told her of his faith in the Savior. He wanted to be invited back, but he knew when the door closed, it would be final. He walked hurriedly across the courtyard by the laughing satyr and came to the bolted door to the outside. The white-haired servant who had admitted him came running to open the door. "Release me from this Babylon," said Barnabas.

VI.

No one was in the street at that time of night. The Temple of Artemis was closed, with only a hint of pink smoke emerging from an opening on the roof. There was no sound except the clop-clop of Olivia's hoofs on the paving stones. Barnabas headed away from the evil house, not caring about direction or destination.

He walked briskly through the chilly night, feeling the benevolent gaze of stars from the bright dome of the heavens. He felt terribly ashamed because he had allowed himself to get involved with the voluptuous woman. He regretted her anger. He wondered if she, like Potiphar's wife, might seek revenge.

Mixed with his shame was a deep feeling of loss. The rabbi, who had come to Cyprus years before, widowed and alone, had depended on him for little kindnesses. He had grown to love and respect his spiritual teacher as a father. He could never forget the impressions the old man had left with him.

Thinking of the help a man can give a boy, Barnabas' thoughts lifted toward Jerusalem and the boy who had watched his donkey, checked daily on his condition, and urged the believers to return to their routine of daily worship. Alone in Jerusalem, after the shipwreck of his family, Jacob was like a piece of jetsam floating in the currents of the sea. He was fortunate to have come in contact with the believers, for they had become a wider family for him, but he needed someone to act as a father. Perhaps I can be that person, if I ever return to Jerusalem, Barnabas thought.

He passed through the sleeping city, and it was like walking through a graveyard with tombs on every side. In the deserted forum and along the paved streets, there were no sounds of life. All Barnabas could hear were Olivia's hoofbeats, and it made him feel that they had come to the end of the world as the only living creatures to face the judgment.

As he approached the beach, he could hear the breakers. He

101

traveled northward, paralleling the coast and the mighty arched aquaduct just inland from the beach.

At a point where the aquaduct leaves the coastline to head toward the hills, he was shocked to hear music. It reminded him of the singers he had heard on that lonely sabbath night walk through Jerusalem. Their celebrating at that time had been understandable—even though it had been contrary to his own mood. But to hear music and celebrating on the beach at dawn was unbelievable.

He drew closer to peer through the coastal fog. He saw a circle of five holy men dancing. Another was playing a stringed instrument. Still another was tending a fire. The black-clad men, with long locks of hair hanging in front of their ears, had arms on each other's shoulders and were skipping first to the right and then to the left. Another unbelievable part was that they had their eyes closed, and their heads swayed back and forth on limber necks. The whole scene was as astounding as rejoicing at a funeral. Barnabus drew still closer, drawn by the spectacle.

"Come and join us," the musician called out.

"No, I don't feel like dancing."

"Join us for our morning meal, then," said the one tending the fire. He was cooking fish.

"If you will let me pay you," said Barnabas.

The five dancers stopped and looked at him. One removed his head covering to wipe perspiration from his forehead. They must have noticed his quizzical expression. "We are praising the Lord, because he has been good to us."

Barnabas asked, "What has made you happy?"

"We have come from Mount Carmel." The name of the place struck the flint of his despondency with a spark. The peak where Elijah had called down fire from heaven in a contest with the priests of Baal would have to be a sacred place, second only to Sinai.

"Where is it?"

"Just over there," said an older man, pointing to the ridge outlined against the sunrise.

102

"So near!" On an impulse, Barnabas said, "Then that is where I am heading. Tell me what to expect."

Each one in the circle, now eating the cooked fish, added some detail. The youngest, or so he seemed from his scraggly beard, mentioned the steep road. Others told of the inspiration they received at the top. The old one spoke slowly. "It has never been a shrine for the crowds. It is a difficult place to get to. I would advise you to ride the donkey."

Again the one with the sparse beard spoke. "That peak has remained a retreat from the world of bargaining and cheating, of revenge and idolatry." Barnabas thanked them and left, refreshed by the pause and enheartened with the prospect of finding some destination for his quest.

With great unrest and agitation, he continued the trip northward to Carmel, that remote peak whose name can excite any believing son of Abraham.

The ass he rode moved too slowly to suit him. He felt like beating some speed into her, but he declined because of her patient, secure progress. He wished he could go straight up the incline, but such a feat was impossible. He tried to content himself with the progress they made on the winding, curving, ever-ascending road-path.

As they went higher, he looked across the cultivated plain, and a cool breeze struck his face. He observed the little green patches of farmland with a fascination; how he loved this good land, this Promised Land. He wished it could remain simple in faith and outlook, uncontaminated by the foreign matter of the world, the scum on the Nile, the Tiber, and the Euphrates.

Impatiently, he requested the ass to go faster, speaking with such phrases of courtesy as "please" and "if possible." His voice sounded unnatural as it echoed back to him from the silence. The pathway became steeper and more filled with weeds. When they reached a level place, some half a mile from the summit, he jumped off the animal and tied her to a tree. He began to take short, fast steps, as he increased the tempo of the journey. But nearing his destination, he slowed down, in order to approach the place with solemnity, instead of breathless impatience that verged on irreverence.

He could see the large rocks on the domed peak, looking as if the entire mountaintop had been fragmented by some long-forgotten catastrophe of nature. In between the boulders, pine trees lifted their sticky needles to the misty atmosphere of the skies. He walked cautiously and finally stopped. To Barnabas, it seemed inappropriate, almost blasphemous to approach a spot, as sacred as the mountain where Moses had met God, with his shoes on, and he paused to slip the sandals from his tired feet. A strong mountain wind, cool and commanding, flowed over the sacred spot. As it blew, thousands of tiny pine needles combed the wind, straightening its sounds into one prolonged gasp of reverence, more eerie than silence.

Barnabas felt near to the God of power, the Almighty who had delivered his people from bondage and who had spoken through his miracle-working prophets, even at this spot sending a lightning flash to consume the drenched altar erected to him. He could never run away from God. He could not forget the sacrifice of Christ and companionship of the church family. He looked down on the fertile plain of Jezreel, asleep in its security, appearing as distant as a childhood memory. The farms and villages of the valley seemed unreal, in contrast to the reality of the sacred, wind-ravished mountain peak. Yet he knew that in those distant houses where people despairing or lusting or plotting rebellion against Rome. The only reality for him at this instant was his Creator's nearness. In a place such as this, anything could happen; no miracle would be too taxing for the Almighty's power.

With arms dangling at his side, Barnabas lifted his head and talked, as if with a friend. "You have given me no answer about Ananias' and Sapphira's deaths. I still don't comprehend. You have not saved the rabbi's life. I cannot understand your ways."

The wind continued to hum. Then he prostrated himself on the rocky dome and said, "O Lord, I will wait for an answer." No flashes of lightning occurred. No voices from the sky sounded. The simple wind blew. The place continued, unconsumed by fire, just as it had for thousands of years. He waited. He concluded that God

104

doesn't deal with all his children in the same way. To some no miracles are granted.

The sun was nearing the horizon. "This place is like a wrestling ring, where Elijah fought Baal. I feel his desire to fight idolatry. I'll return to Jerusalem to see if they will accept me back into the church."

To his back, the sun dropped behind clouds as red as clay pots, and he knew that it was time to leave. He had this day stored in the pit of his soul the spiritual grain that would feed him during times of famine and doubt. He broke off a twig of pine to keep, replaced his sandals, and headed for the waiting animal.

Barnabas returned to the house of the potter. He was excited over the prospect of telling Zadok about the last part of his journey. The potter's place looked strangely quiet. There were no lamps displayed out front. There was no open door to the workroom. He walked along the side alley to the courtyard with its cool kiln and familiar piles of potsherds. There was a smell of emptiness about the place. The bleating of a goat let him know that there was at least one living thing around. He wondered if the animal were hungry, and he, leading Olivia, went back to investigate. He reached out and touched the coarse hair of the goat and saw that she had been milked recently. She didn't look hungry.

"*Shalom,*" said a familiar voice behind him. Jacob, who had sold his services as a donkey-watcher, looked taller now, but he still spoke in a high-pitched voice.

"Zadok said to tell you, when you returned . . ."

"How did he know I would return?" asked Barnabas.

"He said, 'I don't know if it will be next day or next month or next year, but he will return.' "

"He understands me." Barnabas leaned against the cool kiln.

"Sarah does, too."

Barnabas eyed the boy. Then he laughed at the suggestion and thought how much more talkative his young friend had become. Still, however, Jacob was not grown. He was living through that final period of childhood when everything inside the bud wants to push outward, to burst into blossom and fruit.

Barnabas, recalling his own adolescence without a father, said, "I want to help you."

"How?"

"I don't know."

"We were talking about Sarah."

"Were we?" Barnabas could feel his face getting warm. "Where is she now?"

"Tiberius. She has an older sister there. Zadok took her for a visit. He said that he would be back in time to fire the kiln next week. He wants me to help him load it." The boy knelt down in front of the goat and touched his nose to hers. The goat became restless.

"I'm glad Zadok is returning soon. I want to see him."

"Sarah did not want to leave until you returned, Brother Barnabas." The boy moved away from the goat and stood before him, placing both hands on Barnabas' sleeves. He grinned, and Barnabas became as restless as the goat had been. "I think she loves you."

He wished the boy were old enough for him to explain his tangle of feelings and confide in him the unreality of infatuation. He simply said, "She has been very kind to me." He picked up a piece of discarded lamp and tossed it on the sherd pile. The boy still held to him with one hand and waited for him to say more. "She lives the teachings of the Master."

"I wish more of the believers had her charity."

"What do you mean?"

The boy folded his arms in front of him. "Well, some of the people of Jerusalem have not been getting along with the foreign-born believers."

"Ridiculous. I am foreign born," said Barnabas. "You are native born. Yet we get along fine."

"All believers should. This is a time for people to hold together. Have you heard of Saul of Tarsus?"

"No, who is he?"

"I'm not sure, but I have heard that he has sworn to kill all the Followers of the Way. You will have to ask someone else more

106

about him and the danger. This is why Zadok took Sarah away."

"Who could tell me more about this danger?"

"Stephen could. Do you want me to take you to him?"

Barnabas left Olivia and followed the boy to the Synagogue of the Freedmen. It was a large building but not ornate. At the street entrance stood an intelligent-looking young man, who greeted them with the familiar word of peace. Barnabas asked him if Stephen were inside. He had already stated the question before he saw Jacob's signal. Then he learned the reason. The young man tried to answer, "He . . . he . . . he."

"Thank you, we'll find him," said the boy. Inside he explained that the man was called the Babbler. He could say single words like *shalom* and *abba* but he always stuttered over longer statements.

They paused just inside the door and Jacob asked the meaning of a stone engraved in Greek. Barnabas reported, "It says the synagogue, along with its hostelry and cisterns, were built by Theodotus to provide lodging for those from afar." The boy touched the carved sign, running his finger in the groove of the letter "omega." Barnabas looked for the one who would explain the new danger to him.

Then they found Stephen just leaving a group of three men, who were advising him to say no more. "No," he exclaimed. "I plan to come back when Saul is here and prove to him and the others that the Messiah has come."

Barnabas recalled the few eloquent words he had heard from this believer in the upper room before Ananias made his gift. He recalled the harsh words Sapphira had said about him, but he now knew they grew out of her jealousy for attention. As he walked toward them, Barnabas noticed Stephen's eyes were as blue as the zenith of the sky.

"Can you talk with us outside?" asked Barnabas.

"Yes, my brother, you have done so much for the church that I would be glad to do anything you asked." Such words of unlimited promise on the lips of a politician seeking votes would have been incredulous, but from Stephen they sounded like a sacred

107

utterance. Barnabas was grateful that such a believer could set an example for others. As they were leaving the synagogue door, the Babbler was there, smiling expectantly. He grabbed Stephen by the sleeve. *"Shalom,* my brother," Stephen said and paused to look at him.

"Thank you for that word of peace," responded the surprised Babbler. "It is easy for me to talk to you." He seemed to realize that he was not stammering.

Jacob said, "See if you can talk to someone else. Maybe you are healed."

Barnabas, hearing the remark, wished his faith were as spontaneous as the boy's, and he waited to see. At that time a salesman with a full waterskin strapped across his back came along the street. The young man said, "How much do you charge for a drink of water?"

Before the seller could answer, the boy shouted to the crowd, "Stephen has cured the Babbler." People came running from every direction and quickly formed a compact circle around the happy speaker.

"Not I, but the Messiah did this."

Barnabas grabbed Stephen, "This is a miracle of healing."

Stephen answered modestly, "This is a small event. When Peter walks out in the street, paralytics are cured when his shadow falls on them. He is an apostle; I am only a follower."

The water seller, with strident voice, was yelling to others on the edge of the crowd, and women in second-story windows were screaming back and forth the exciting news. It became impossible to converse. Stephen whispered something in the ear of the healed man and led Barnabas and Jacob from the pushing crowd.

They stopped at a place' where animals were drinking from a trough. It was comparatively quiet, and Stephen told them of the extreme danger that awaited Followers of the Way. "I am afraid that all who remain here will be exterminated; perhaps some will turn back to the ways of the world. But we must not be surprised, for the servant is not better than his master. We must expect suffering, and fear nothing in the world but the temptations of the devil." His words were spellbinding, and there seemed to be an

108

aura about his face as he spoke of suffering.

Barnabas asked his advice. "Would it be cowardice for an older believer to leave Jerusalem until the danger passes over?"

"No, a believer could prolong his life and make it count as a witness in another place. It might be a great blessing if our believers will scatter."

"I am grateful, Stephen. Now I must go."

Stephen said, *"Shalom."*

Barnabas thought he had never heard the word more beautifully said. It seemed to carry with it a high priestly blessing. Inspired, yet cautiously he headed for the potter's place.

Barnabas knew what he must do. He wanted to leave for Tiberius immediately. He wanted to stop Zadok before he returned to the Holy City. Perhaps the old man could live there in safety with his two granddaughters. He went by the house, took Olivia, and said farewell to Jacob.

The trip to Tiberius was uneventful. He found Zadok without any trouble. Barnabas kissed both him and Sarah. She was too embarrassed to say anything. But the old potter talked of returning to his wheel and kiln. Even when Barnabas offered to transfer all his equipment to this beautiful new city on the Sea of Galilee, the old man would not consider the proposal. Instead, he took Barnabas on a tour of Tiberius. As he showed him where to sell pottery lamps, Barnabas realized that Zadok was commissioning him to take the place of Ananias. In order to help his benefactor, Barnabas promised that he would distribute the lamps, if he did not have to make any trips to Caesarea. The old man chewed his lips but did not ask why. When they had agreed on plans, they returned to Jerusalem, with Zadok riding Olivia and Barnabas leading.

Barnabas found a confused situation when they returned. John Mark told him that the day after he left, Stephen had returned to debate in the synagogue. When he enraged the congregation by calling them murderers of the Righteous One, they took him before the Sanhedrin. Then Barnabas learned, with the familiar pangs of grief gripping his heart, that they had stoned Stephen to death. But everyone reported that his face had been like an angel's. On the day of Stephen's death, a severe persecution had started, led by the fanatic legalist from Tarsus, Saul.

Zadok refused to work, when they returned, but he spent several days visiting the homes of the believers. Barnabas, growing impatient with him, said to the boy, "If Zadok were not going to return to his work, he should have remained in safe Tiberius."

Jacob replied bluntly, "Don't criticize him. Zadok is doing this for you."

"What can he do for me in the houses of the members?"

"He can tell them that you did not desert him and Sarah because you were frightened. The people have been talking a lot. Some of the gossips make up things to keep their minds off their own fears." Barnabas said nothing. He was stunned, although he had wondered if the believers would accept him back into the congregation. Finally, Jacob questioned his silence: "Are you angry?"

"No, I am not angry at these people. They had a right to talk. They were correct about my desertion, but they were wrong about my cowardice. Whatever the cause, I am grateful that Zadok wanted to give me a second chance. If I ever have the opportunity to give a person a second chance, I will."

All appeared to be unity and understanding in the dwindling church fellowship. But one night at the table, Barnabas sat near James, the brother of Jesus, who said, "The believers are becoming too loose. We need more strictness."

"But Jesus taught us . . ."

With vehemence he responded, "I know what he taught. He said that he came to fulfil the law, not destroy it." The authoritarian tone had silenced any discussion on the topic, yet he was unwilling to stop. "Stephen once made a dangerous suggestion about the unimportance of the Temple. I believe that Peter is catching some of this same liberal disease."

"No, my brother, didn't Jesus cleanse the Temple, showing his disappointment with it?" Barnabas asked the question, with the

110

turbulent memories of his own disenchantment tumbling beneath the surface.

Like a hammer hitting a nail, James brought his hand down on the table, shaking the bowl of milk curd until some spilled out. "No, Jesus loved the Temple so much that he was willing to suffer misunderstanding in order to cleanse it. He wanted it pure and clean, like a virgin for her groom."

A person who had become more embittered than the rest said, "But she was more like a whore."

James stood up, with his face reddened, his nostrils distended, and the veins running down his neck throbbing. "Enough of this blasphemy. We are Jews. We are not mongrels who worship in Samaria." Someone tried to interrupt, no doubt to point out the flourishing work in Samaria, but the co-head of the church continued. "It is true that my brother talked to a woman of Samaria, but he did not call her as one of his disciples. It is true that he said he had other sheep. But if he were still preaching today, he would expect these would-be followers to become Jews first, then his disciples."

Barnabas could not keep his mind on the argument. His mouth was salivating, as if he had eaten spoiled meat. It was sickening to hear followers of the Prince of Peace carry on in such a bellicose way. He pushed back from the table, and he headed for the door. He stepped outside and paused at the steps, the same ones which had borne the weight of Ananias and Sapphira. These same steps, Barnabas thought, must have held the Teacher's sorrowful feet as they trudged away from that final supper.

The step behind him creaked, and he looked back to see his cousin. "Is anything wrong?" asked John Mark.

"No, I must get away to think."

"Are you thinking of giving up the faith?"

"No, Mark, I have already made up my mind on that matter. My biggest problem is with people who call themselves followers, but walk in such a different way from Jesus."

"I, too, have worried over this. But Peter told me . . ." Mark's voice mounted in vigor as he mentioned the name of the great

111

fisherman. "Peter told me I should never put my faith in other people, or I would surely be disappointed. I should put my faith in Jesus only."

"Will you come to my room?"

Barnabas accepted, relieved that the youth had sensed his need. He followed John Mark into a room that was twice the size of the room at Zadok's. Everything was as neat as a sea captain's cabin. The bed was wrinkle free. Near the window stood a writing table. The most fascinating thing about the tidy room was a collection of scrolls. Along one entire wall there was a honeycomb of shelves. In each compartment was a scroll with an identifying tag hanging from it. One scroll lay partially open on the table.

Barnabas, surprised to see such a collection apart from an academy or a wealthy synagogue, said, "Where did you get these?"

"I was training to be a scribe, when I gave my life to the Savior. I continued in the scribal school until I could stand the students' jeers no longer. My mother was able to buy these papyrus scrolls and two parchment books from the estate of a teacher. Now I work on this project every day but the sabbath." His eyes gleamed. "I have time for nothing else."

"Mark, what would happen to the church if Peter were imprisoned or put to death?"

"I guess we would have to depend on some miracle of revelation."

When Barnabas realized that Mark did not see what he was trying to point out, he said, "No miracle is needed—just your work redirected." He saw the young man's mouth drop open in disbelief. "Your work with the Scriptures could be done . . ." He wanted to add "by any scribe at anytime," but he simply said, "later."

"You are asking me to quit my work?"

"No, instead of working with the prophets of old, write down the main events in the life of Jesus." The young man looked away toward the blank wall opposite the scrolls and seemed to be looking through the plaster and stones. Barnabas said, "Listen to Peter. Write down his exact words; he makes sure that they are always the same. No one else has recorded these recollections, and two

112

years from now might be too late."

Mark grabbed his arm and said, "I brought you here to help you." His face was flushed. "You have hurt me, when all I intended was to help you. You have received no advice, but you have cast doubt on my study of the expectations of the Messiah. Do you realize that these scrolls are worth a small fortune?"

"Of course, I do. I still say you can return to them. But pray about this matter, John Mark, and see if the Lord leads you to preserve the exact words of the Teacher. Maybe the Lord will send us together to some place like Cyprus where people hunger for words such as Jesus gave."

Just before Barnabas closed the door, the young man asked, "Away from Jerusalem?"

Severe persecutions gave way to minor harrassments. Sarah returned to Jerusalem, and repeated the rumor that Saul had repented. Barnabas believed the story, but others called it another of the fanatic's tricks to catch the unwary. On regular trips to Tiberius to distribute lamps, Barnabas frequently heard the name of Saul, but he could discover nothing about his activities.

Each time he returned to his Jerusalem home, Barnabas could see changes in his friends. Time was a capricious thief, taking strength away from Zadok and giving it to Jacob. Barnabas said to Sarah, "If God should lead me away from Jerusalem forever, please take care of the boy for me."

Although a cloud of sadness passed over her face, she smiled and said, "Yes, Brother Barnabas." She understood everything he meant.

In his second year of delivering lamps, Barnabas visited Scythopolis, an ancient city once known as Beth Shan, where the desecrated bodies of King Saul and Jonathan had hung on its walls in defeat. When he completed his business, the Cypriot visited the basilica of the law. The followers of Christ met there because they had been excluded from the synagogue. In the large congregation, Barnabas thought he saw a Roman soldier. Perhaps he or one of his friends officiated at the crucifixion, the new Christian thought as he prayed to keep from hating the foreigner.

113

After the psalms and prayers had ended, the soldier stood up to speak. He looked like someone Barnabas had known in his past. He spoke. "I am Julius of the Augustan Cohort. I am a seeker not an enemy." Barnabas felt his palms grow cold and clammy. The situation was unbelievable. he had doubted the prospects of seeing this man again. He had prayed for him. Now he stared at the Roman, wondering what kind of announcement he was about to make to the church.

"Friends, I would like to become one of you." Barnabas began to experience the same dream-like feeling he had felt when he saw Stephen heal the Babbler. "For a long time I have looked for some meaning in life. I did not find it from the myths of Greece or Rome. I did not find it from the Jews I met in Alexandria or along the highways of Judea." Barnabas swallowed and recalled his own confused mind when they had traveled together toward Jerusalem.

The soldier continued, "I want to know if I can become a believer. Or must I become a Jew first and then a follower of Christ?" Barnabas, like the others in the meeting, blinked in amazement. It was the first time Barnabas had heard the query, and he did not dream that this same question would plague his work for the rest of his life.

A middle-aged leader stood up to answer. "Have you ever taken lessons as a proselyte or been circumcized?"

"No, I know little of your Scriptures, except the commandments. I am not interested in Moses and Abraham, but I am interested in the story of Jesus' life and death. I believe my Roman world will suffocate in cruelty and in lust unless we turn to the teachings of the Nazarene."

Twilight softened the colors in the basilica, but Barnabas felt the radiance of noon. The leader, still standing, asked, "How did you learn of Jesus' life and teachings?"

"From believers in Damascus."

"I speak for the congregation when I say that we are glad you are a seeker. I must admit that I don't know the answer to your question. We must refer it to the apostles in Jerusalem for an authoritative answer."

114

"I will not be able to remain here for the news. My work will take me away tomorrow morning. But I will keep seeking to learn more of Christ in my travels. I hope that I will be able to maintain my work as a courier without being called on to kill or break any of God's other commands. Please, pray for me."

In the informal service, several men responded, "We will."

Barnabas, feeling almost intoxicated, listened as the soldier continued. "I bring you good news from Damascus, from which I have just returned on official business. Saul, who tormented some of you in Jerusalem, has been a believer for many months. He has been off to meditate and pray. Now he is again in Damascus, teaching with such fervor that the synagogue leaders are infuriated. His life is in grave danger. I hope that some plan can be devised for him to escape, but already paid killers wait at the gates of the city. Pray for him. If God should miraculously spare him and send him in this direction, receive him as a brother."

Others with less restraint than Barnabas filled the basilica with shouts of celebration. Some prayed aloud. Others sang. The soldier walked out, and Barnabas rushed past the door to meet him. Julius did not immediately recognize Barnabas, but when he did, he threw both arms about him. The squeeze equaled that of any wrestler Barnabas had ever encountered. They went outside, where the evening star had just appeared.

The former traveling companions talked for hours. Then, when they finally realized that they must bring their reunion to an end, Barnabas asked one more question: "What is Saul like?"

"You have never seen anyone to equal him. He is like a person whose clothes have caught fire. He is in a frenzy to do what he feels is the important thing of the moment. He wants to teach and to testify before the fire consumes him. I hope that God will spare him so that you can hear him."

"I would do anything to meet him and hear him. If he comes to Jerusalem, I will introduce him to the scoffers. I want them to see the power of God in a changed life." Barnabas realized that he had raised his voice in excitement. "I'd like to bring him not only to people here in Scythopolis but also to Tiberius and even

115

to Antioch."

"Would you stop there?" asked Julius as he walked away.

Suddenly, Barnabas was alone but not lonely, feeling the yearn for travel as strong as a pang of hunger. He tried to envision his future as he hurried back to seething Jerusalem.

It was the middle of the hot season, and storks were migrating from lands south of Egypt to places beyond Carmel. Everything seemed in turmoil throughout the land. Rumors multiplied about a band of revolutionaries living in the Judean hills, and some Sadducees claimed the insurgents were followers of Christ. Gossips alleged that believers secretly worshiped an ass's head. In the confused times, prisoners were transferred from one citadel to another.

Barnabas went to talk with Peter. The fisherman spoke before Barnabas could state his purpose. "Please tell your cousin to give me some rest. He has squeezed my mind like an olive in a press. I can give him no more recollections."

"You have been patient with Mark." Barnabas had never seen Peter this irritable before, and he blamed the combination of age and responsibility.

"Yes, but my patience has come to an end. He insists that I tell him more, but I refuse to speak of an incident that occurred when I was not present or relate some teaching that has grown vague in my memory. If I cannot quote it exactly, I refuse to guess at it."

"You are right, Peter, and I'm sure that Mark will understand."

"I have not been able to get him to see it, but maybe you can. He is a persistent man." Barnabas smiled because Peter had not used the word "boy." He was glad to hear that his cousin could stick with a task.

"Peter, Zadok is growing weaker."

"I have not seen him at the services in several weeks. I have been concerned but have not had time to visit him."

"He stumbles and falls. He has been unable to cook his meals while I have been away. He has lost much weight, and he does not want to inconvenience the widows by asking them to bring him his food."

116

"They would be glad to do it, Barnabas, especially for this one who has done so much for many of us."

"Last week, he went out in the street toward the hippodrome. He stumbled. Just at that time the high priest was making an excursion into the lower city to learn what he could for making charges of blasphemy. Zadok fell right at his feet."

"I had not heard of this. What happened?"

Barnabas said, "The high priest actually bent over and helped him up. He did not say anything about the law, but he warned Zadok to be careful. When Sarah learned of this incident, she insisted on moving back, regardless of the danger. She returned today."

"She is a brave young woman. Can we help with money from the church treasury?" Peter walked to the door to make sure no one was listening.

"No, we are able to make a good living from the lamp business, although Zadok is not working. The boy is doing the work."

"Did his grandmother really expell him from her household because of his faith?"

"Yes, but it has worked out to be a blessing for Zadok and his business. Maybe Sarah, Zadok, and I can give the boy the . . ."

They were interrupted by a visitor. A man with a middle-aged belly, a converted Jew who introduced himself as a cloth seller from Damascus, said he had a message. When he handed the scrap of papyrus to Peter, the rough fisherman's hands tore it up. Barnabas wondered what message could be so unimportant or so irritating that Peter would destroy it. The apostle had ripped the little note to shreds in front of the messenger. "If he is really a Follower, he should have stayed in Damascus. He can do nothing here."

When he said the name of the city, Damascus, Barnabas guessed the identity of the person. It must be Saul of Tarsus. When the persecutor had first gone to that great city in Syria, people had gossiped about his change of mind. Nowadays, he was hardly mentioned. He had been away for three years. There were more serious dangers to speak of and more illustrious Followers to talk

117

about.

The messenger shrugged his shoulder, almost as if he expected such a response, and walked out. Peter said, "If you held the responsibility I do, you'd have done the same thing. Besides, James . . ."

"Peter, my brother, do whatever you think is right. But get the facts before you make an impulsive decision."

"Barnabas"—tears glistened in his eyes—"you know—everybody knows—the mistakes I've made by blurting out the first idea that came to my mind." Peter, the leading apostle and greatest threat to the high priest, laid a heavy hand on the Cypriot's shoulder for support. "I am willing to get more facts."

"Good. I'll find out what I can for you." Barnabas walked out a door, the rusty hinges of which squeaked a warning. As he left the old fisherman, he turned his mind from Saul and thought of the potter's house. There four believers under one roof appeared to be a family of mother, father, child, and grandfather. He wondered how long he could help to hold these together in the storm of misunderstanding that was blowing.

Walking through the swarming city, he thought of how people had turned against one another like snarling dogs. The boy had been thrown out of his grandmother's house. Sometimes a church member would be called up before the high priest or the Sanhedrin, wondering which of his friends had informed the Jewish leaders of his membership. Old friendships disintegrated under the pressure of suspicion. The Followers of the Way were finding it difficult to walk in the footsteps of the Savior. It was not easy to continue as a believer. He wondered if Saul's presence could possibly help, and he prayed most of the night.

The first morning after Sarah's return, the four gathered around the table to eat a light meal. Sarah had rested from her trip, and the old man and boy engaged in a contest of yawning and stretching. After Barnabas led in prayer, no one talked. There was much

118

to be said. He needed to warn Sarah about danger. She needed to know the things that had happened in the church since she had departed for Tiberius.

Finally, the boy, his mouth mush-filled, said, "Today I will load the kiln. I am proud of myself. Every lamp in the batch I made myself, without any help."

Sarah said, "Jacob, you have grown a handsbredth taller."

Barnabas, who was with the boy constantly, even sleeping in the same room with him, now looked at his growth in amazement. He was not the same lad who had first spotted him at the Temple. The time had already come for him to be made a Son of the Covenant; yet with the current turmoil, nothing had been done about the ceremony. He no longer looked nor talked like a child.

As if to disprove Sarah's words and Barnabas' thoughts, Jacob told of making a lamp the previous day that had swelled up as large as a boat. The growing boy still enjoyed telling Sarah the most incredible stories because she always believed them. He did not try them on Barnabas, except for one time when he had told him that the almond tree in the courtyard was producing silver shekels. Hoping for a miracle, Barnabas had raced to the tree to find nothing but disappointing leaves as thin as skin. After that he believed none of the boy's tales and tried to get Sarah to ask him a second time before she believed him.

Another time Jacob had claimed that he found two snakes in the potter's shop. They got so angry that they ate each other up. Barnabas tried not to snicker. When Sarah demanded proof, he showed her the empty shop. "If it were a lie, one snake would be left."

Sarah said, "I must clean up the loom and thread it."

Zadok said slowly, "I must make my preparation for death."

"No, my friend," said Barnabas. "You must prepare to live. I will go after clay today. When you see it, you will want to return to your wheel." Zadok chewed his lip and let his eyelids drop until they were half closed. It was not possible to tell if he were awake or asleep.

Barnabas whispered to Sarah, "Watch him closely. We must not

119

let him fall. A broken hip kills more elderly people than anything I know of. Do you want me to stay with you today and go after clay another day?"

Jacob answered, "The clay cannot wait."

Barnabas, surprised, said, "I think of it as the other way around. The clay can wait indefinitely; it will be there a year from now. But. . ." He did not finish the sentence, and he did not finish the meal. As he acquiesced to the youth's wishes, he watched the boy stride toward the workshop. Barnabas, knowing that he needed to start the clay, left his aged friend with one he considered the best nurse in Judea, making two requests: "Be careful, and pray that God will lead me to Brother Saul."

His errand carried him past the pool of Bethesda and out the Sheep Gate, on the north side of the city. Just outside the opened gates, he saw a caravan of camels and donkeys camped. The animals were standing close by the tents of the camel drivers. Numerous bundles, which had been carried across hot dusty trails on the backs of the camels, were now stacked in large piles. A few of the packages had been opened, perhaps to display to prospective buyers.

He recognized one of the leading merchants from the bazaar area in Jerusalem walking in and out among the stacks of merchandise. Then Barnabas noticed that the local citizen was being led by a paunchy little man who looked familiar. He pondered. Suddenly, he knew it was the same one who had delivered the note to Peter the previous day. The two men began to argue over prices, and a half-circle of children formed around them to listen.

Barnabas pushed through them. "May I interrupt?" Both men looked relieved. The day was still new, and the haggling had just started; they welcomed an interruption. "I want to see him. Where is he?"

In the fierce glare of the dealer's eyes, Barnabas knew that he had asked a dangerous question. Then the man's eyes relaxed in their slits, and he smilingly said, "I am glad you inquired, but you can see I am busy now. The tentmaker you wish to see will show you his wares this afternoon."

120

Barnabas was angry—not at the caravan leader—with himself. He had almost disclosed to a leading Jewish merchant the stunning news of the renegade's return. Just such a thoughtless act could spark another slaughter, a useless martyrdom. Jerusalem could be more dangerous for Saul than it had been for Stephen and others who had died because of their apparent disregard of the law. Barnabas lingered near the Sheep Gate and sat inconspicuously with a figcake salesman in a shadow. While eating figs and popping the tiny seeds between his teeth, he kept his eye on the caravan leader, who with another prospective customer, was sitting in the shade of a tent; they were drinking from Syrian goblets. The day grew hotter, and the figcake salesman became more inquisitive. Just when Barnabas was ready to return to the potter's shop for something to drink, the customer left.

Barnabas went to the leader, apologized for his dangerous interruption of the morning, and asked to see Saul of Tarsus.

"There he is." The Syrian pointed to an insignificant person sitting cross-legged near the camels, wearing a robe so near the color of the animals that he could have ridden across the desert and other caravans would have thought they had seen a stray camel without a rider. He was looking toward the walls of the Holy City.

"It cannot be."

The leader said, "Yes, he escaped the trap they laid for him in Damascus. It was a miraculous delivery." They started walking in Saul's direction.

Only when they stood directly in front of him did the man from Tarsus take his eyes from the walls of Jerusalem and stand up to greet them. The former persecutor did not look at all as Barnabas had expected. He was not large and fierce. He looked like an ordinary camel driver or cloth merchant. He was short and balding.

"I am Joseph of Cyprus, now called Barnabas."

Saul echoed the name, "Barnabas, Son of Encouragement, one who accompanies and brings comfort. All morning I have prayed for the chance to meet you. Peace." When he smiled, there was a space between his two front teeth. The only hint of intensity was

121

in his eyes; now he fixed his gaze on Barnabas. As if he were chanting a funeral prayer, Saul said, "I do not feel wanted here. The church is afraid of me, or else they will not forgive me."

The words triggered a denial on the lips of Barnabas. He explained that the church did not know of his presence, and from the short note he had received, Peter did not comprehend the situation.

The two new acquaintances moved away from the smelly camels and found some shade under an olive tree. Barnabas asked what had changed Saul's life and heard an unbelievable story. The former persecutor began in a whisper and told of his errand to Damascus. "Every mile of that 140-mile trip was torture. I was persecuting myself more than I was the Followers. I did everything I knew to erase from my memory the golden voice of Stephen—to forget his angelic—but failed. I despised myself. I prayed that God would hurl a bolt of lightning to kill me. He answered my prayer. He answered!" Saul raised his voice so loud that the caravan leader turned from a customer and stared.

More quietly, he resumed, "He destroyed my old life. From the thunder I heard Christ's voice. I learned that I had been hurting his body, the church. The Head cried out from heaven." The converted persecutor shared the exciting story of his blindness and told how Ananias came to lay on his hands and related the thrill of his baptism.

Apologetically Barnabas responded, "My conversion was quite different. I was tired and worn out from my sickness, and the trip down to the Jordan left me completely exhausted. It was not the same thrill you mentioned, but the Way has given me meaning to life and becomes more thrilling to travel each year."

Saul had a strange answer: "Aside from your illness, I suspect that you joined this group like you would a group that sits around a courtyard at nightfall, to fill the needs of your loneliness."

Barnabas felt his face growing hot, as if it were sunburned. He knew other immigrants who had joined the believers for such reasons, but he had never considered his own actions in that light. He was too embarrassed to deny Saul's guess. He explained, "My first thoughts were to fill up my loneliness with friends. Now I have learned to put my emphasis on the Master, not on his followers —on the Shepherd, and not on the sheep."

Saul, not condemning, said, "Your words remind me of Stephen."

Both Barnabas and Saul said no more but became quiet. Barnabas wondered if the persecutor were thinking of Stephen's forceful words that led to his tragic but beautiful death. Barnabas knew he would always be grateful for his acquaintance with the martyr, one of God's heroes. Then Saul shattered the silence with a simple request: "I want to view the chief pillar of the church; take me to Peter."

At their meeting Peter showed none of the impetuosity that had caused him to tear up the note, and Saul revealed none of the despondency that had made him feel persecuted even by the church. The conversation went so well that Peter invited the visitor to share his simple accommodations for several days. He was especially impressed with the Damascus Road experience, and he wanted others to hear.

When word got around that Saul would make a speech, almost as many people gathered to hear him as had assembled to hear Peter the time he was miraculously released from prison. Everyone talked of the great change that had come over the legalistic tyrant.

The days stretched into a week. Some people heard of Saul's presence and came to stare at him. Others, with little of the spirit of the Christ they professed to follow, warned that if he came to the upper room, they would get up and walk out. One person sent word that if Saul did not leave, he would set fire to Peter's house.

At first the two laughed about the misunderstanding, but then Saul confided to Barnabas, if he remained, he might displace some of the high priest's wrath from himself to the believers and cause them to suffer. They set a day to leave, but a strange set of circumstances forced a delay.

Jerusalem smoldered with hostility. Someone in the high priest's family had been walking near the walls of the city, when a stone fell on his head. It must have been an accident, but the high priest claimed that believers were retaliating.

Sarah, who had learned about these matters as she went for water, suggested a delay in Saul's departure. She advised Saul and Barnabas to stay inside the closed shop. "It is the day of the funeral procession. People will be more agitated than usual. They might turn to looting."

Barnabas agreed, but the boy saw no reason to close up. It did not suit his plans. "If I were actually his father, I would forbid him to open up tomorrow," Barnabas said after Jacob went out to play.

"You are more like a brother to him," Sarah said, in a way that sounded critical. "When I was a child, we obeyed my father. He was strict."

Barnabas knew that Sarah was right in praising strictness, yet she herself should have been stern. She had known him longer.

While Barnabas was working with the kiln, he heard a noise from the front of the shop. Saul had called a part of his name. The way he stopped alarmed the man at the oven, who dropped several lamps that were ready for firing.

He rushed to the front workroom, with its door opening on to the street and the merchandise display there. As he entered the back door, he paused long enough to blink his eyes at the situation.

He saw three strangers. They were not quite men, but certainly not children. He assumed that these eighteen- or nineteen-year-olds had been in the funeral procession and had become incited over the mysterious death. Now, with no work to do for the rest of the day, they had decided to terrorize believers. He saw Saul lying on the floor unconscious. He got to the door as the three of them advanced toward the helpless lad. The middle one, taller than the others, grabbed at the boy with his left hand, ripping off his mud-splattered apron, and drew back his right hand to slap him across the head.

Seeing Saul and Jacob in trouble released a catapult in his mind.

124

He did not hesitate, even though it had been years since he had fought. There was no time for a plan. He simply lurched at the bully. Barnabas had forgotten that he possessed a boiling temper.

He had muscles trained for fighting, and he knew how to use them. Still virile and strong, he had once wrestled the champion of Cyprus (in private, because he refused to compete publicly for the championship; he would not disgrace himself, his mother, and his race by appearing naked in public).

He jerked the leader off the helpless victim as he would snatch a fox off a rabbit. He pushed him against another of the advancing youths. When the third one grabbed the boy, Barnabas lifted the hoodlum into the air and tossed him, stumbling and rolling across the floor, shaking the wall so hard that three kiln-dried lamps fell to the floor. Because of their hardness, two did not break, but one lamp cracked apart. The boy stood with his fingers stretched out like paws, ready to claw the next one to come near him.

The two repulsed bullies advanced together. Barnabas raised his voice in a loud, menacing roar. The surprising noise stopped the charging fighters. The third one cut his eyes around, as if he were looking for a place to run. Continuing to scream judgments on the trio, Barnabas raised his arm. When the third one realized his danger, he ducked the thrashing arm and ran. The other two followed his example. As they withdrew, Barnabas lifted his heavy voice in a final warning. Afterwards he stood in the doorway panting. Saul stirred.

The boy, no longer a baby, did not run to his arms but squatted on the floor, daubing at his bloodied knees. His great brown eyes revealed the appreciation that his lips could not utter.

A presence, a slender figure in the back door, like an Egyptian mummy, said in a flute-like voice, "That is not the Way Jesus taught."

"I know," Barnabas responded. He sat on the floor by Saul and found that his visitor was not seriously hurt. He asked, "Brother Saul, were you afraid?"

There was an agitated tone to his answer, and the whites of his eyes glistened. "Not once. I had nothing to be afraid of. I was in similar danger in Damascus. But my Christ has some mighty work for me to do, and he will preserve me to do it."

After the evening meal, the others were tired and went to bed. Barnabas sat at the table thinking. He had supposed that the Way would be straight and traversable, like the best Roman highway. Instead, he was finding it filled with impediments and offering frequent sidepaths and crossroads. Following the Way did not solve all his problems; indeed, it created more. He wondered if he might ever be called on to die for his faith, like Stephen.

Barnabas could not go to sleep. He heard a quiet sobbing coming from the boy's bed. While he was wondering if he might embarrass Jacob by going to him, the tentmaker stood up and shouted, "I must return to Tarsus."

"Tomorrow," said Barnabas. "You need some rest. Perhaps tomorrow night will. . ."

"No, Now."

Barnabas, along with Mark and a cheesemaker neighbor, accompanied Saul to the familiar seaport of Caesarea. As they passed the House of the Laughing Satyr, Barnabas felt a peculiar tangle of feelings. He led them to the busy quay, where sailors had begun to loosen the ropes on a ship laden with amphorae of olive oil. One of the lines carried a wharf rat on its way to the ship, but the rodent held to the loosened rope, refusing to fall into the water, ready to work his destruction on the vessel. The cheesemaker and Mark said farewell and moved back toward the warehouse arches, leaving the two by the vessel.

Barnabas wondered how Saul would express his appreciation. He had not done a lot for the tentmaker, but he had introduced him to the apostles, encouraged him in his speaking, and safely accompanied him to the Tarsus-bound ship. For a time Saul said nothing. When the captain shouted, he said gravely, "The Lord has used you to save me for his work. The time will come when you will feel God leading you to come get me to help you in his work. I will be ready. *Shalom.*."

Barnabas watched the vessel slide away, almost as stunned as he had been by the impact of that beam from long ago on the

126

Temple bridge. He thought of a new mission in life, and he was no longer restless. The idea, like the waters of baptism, rolled over him, and he shouted across the water, *"Shalom."*